THERE'S SOMETHING IN THE WOODS

MOLLY LIKOVICH

For Ashley and Eric. Thank you for helping me survive the worst days of my life. I hope wherever you are you're all right.

"I went out to the hazel wood because a fire was in my head."

— WILLIAM BUTLER YEATS

IMPORTANT NOTE FROM THE AUTHOR

Although the story you are about to read of Jay Dove and her daring escape from an evil mental hospital is fiction, the trauma she suffers in the hospital is all based loosely on my own time in a mental hospital that abused its patients, myself included. This story delves deep into topics of PTSD from mental health malpractice and abuse, as well as suicidal ideation, and explicit violence and gore. It may not be suitable for all readers, so please take care of your own mental health and proceed with caution.

GLOSSARY OF WEATHER TERMS

Anabatic Wind: An upslope wind usually applied only when the wind is blowing up hill or mountain as the result of local surface heating, and apart from the effects of the larger scale circulation.

Anvil: Elongated cloud at the top of the storm that spreads downwind with upper level steering winds.

Dereco: A very long lived and damaging thunderstorm.

Hook Echo: A hook echo is a pendant or hook-shaped weather radar signature as part of some supercell thunderstorms.

PLAYLIST

Weight of Living - Bastille
Quarter Past Midnight - Bastille
I'm Gonna Show You Crazy - Bebe Rexha
sick to my stomach - emily jeffri
Cloudbusting - Kate Bush
Mad Hatter - Emily Martinez
ALICE -PEGGY
Villainous Things - Shayfer James
evermore - Taylor Swift (feat. Bon Iver)
No Plan - Sophia Anne Caruso
Out Of The Woods (Taylor's Version) - Taylor Swift
Flight Risk - Tommy Lefroy
Achilles Come Down - Gang of Youths
Carolina - Taylor Swift
Heavy - Peach PRC
Lil' Red Riding Hood - Amanda Seyfried
Winter of Our Youth - Bastille
Wonderland (Taylor's Version) - Taylor Swift
Walking in the Air - Karliene

White Rabbit - Jefferson Airplane
Pure As The Driven Snow - Rachel Zegler
Safe & Sound - Taylor Swift
Snow Angel - Reneé Rapp

FLURRIES

This might not be the best time to remember that I'm a terrible driver. Ten minutes ago, now that would've been the *perfect* time to remember. Not now, on ice slick roads, in a car I've never been behind the wheel of before, my spine nothing but a collection of burning spasms, and snowfall coming down harder and harder with every passing minute. But ten minutes ago this was the only option. The only means of escape.

Nurse Ann is an idiot. She shouldn't always be leaving her keys by the computer at the front desk if she didn't want one of us crazies to take them. She shouldn't have made her car so easy to spot with its array of conservative bumper stickers that match her disgusting views. And she shouldn't have been such an absolute, total, evil cunt to me and everyone else if she didn't want me to stab her hand with a pencil that one time a week ago.

It doesn't matter why I did it. She deserved it.

Everyone agrees with me.

It was worth it to see the horrified looks on her nursing students' faces.

Serves them right too, talking to us like we were a bunch of dancing monkeys at a carnival.

I can't think about any of that now though. I need to think about the road, focus on the road, and not running off it.

I take a sharp turn just as the sound of sirens creeps up behind me. They're only a few miles away, they'll be on me soon and then I don't know what I'll do. I'm not going back. Ever. I'd rather die. Rather go to prison. Rather stab myself with a pencil. Anything to avoid the worst eight months of my life ever repeating. I just have to get back home. Get to my sister. She can work all of this out. When my parents brought me in they told them it would just be a 48 hour hold. And now they've been lying to my family about what my behavior has been like while I was there. All for dear old Dad's fancy insurance. But Katrina is a lawyer. She will believe me and she will fix this.

It's just a five hour drive.

I can get there.

I *will* get there. Through hell or high water.

Or a fucking blizzard.

Or my body working against me.

As if on cue, a spasm makes its way into my neck and I twitch as the pain hisses through me. I black out for a moment, my eyes going hazy. Thankfully I come back to my senses quickly enough to stay on the road.

The sirens are getting louder. My chest burns with panic, my cheeks flush despite the cold I'm grossly unprepared for. Stanley gave me his coat when I told him my plan. It's big which helps for warmth, being able to snuggle inside it like a blanket but not so much for easy and smooth mobility. My gross, paper pajamas crinkle beneath me. I can already feel several tears in the cheap fabric. And my feet. My stupid feet. I didn't exactly want to run out in nothing but my grippy socks, but my boots have no laces, so they're just flopping around on my feet. Stupid rules, as if I could hang myself with shoelaces. I don't even know how to tie a noose.

The sirens are so loud now.

I need to focus.

My bad driving catches up to me when I hit a patch of black ice and panic. I can't remember if I'm supposed to steer into or away from the skidding. My fear takes over and I turn away. This was clearly the wrong move. Ann's ugly car spins out up onto a snowbank at the edge of the woods, sending my face crashing against the steering wheel as the car smokes and stalls out. The seat belt chokes me, a red welt painting itself across my throat, tearing into my paper clothing. I feel blood trickle down my face. I gingerly touch my forehead where a gash now covers half the area.

Great.

Just great.

I can't stay here.

I open the driver's side door and practically fall out, my palms making sharp contact with the icy asphalt. I gasp from the pain as I struggle to my feet. My back decides it's time to go back into spasm. Half a dozen fists clench throughout the muscles in my back, parcheesi dice rattle up and down my spine, playing a painful tune with every tap. My jaw goes slack as the waves of agony roll through me. Fuck them for taking my cane. Another thing to add to the very long list of why I hate that place and every staff member in it.

I grip the open car door to get my balance, gritting my teeth, trying to slow my breathing. I slide a hand in my pocket to make sure the folded up piece of paper is still there. I'm brought to a miniscule moment of peace when my fingertips brush against the worn sudoku sheet. Once the pain has subsided enough that it doesn't hurt to inhale, I take off into the woods. I run as fast as I can, pumping my arms, trying to pick my feet up with my loose boots in the ever deepening snow. My spine burns, my chest constricts, and I'm so dizzy from the incessant fatigue that the forest tilts around me. I feel like a demented version of Alice and this nightmare is my Wonderland. The sound of sirens is fading into the background the further into the woods I run but I can feel my fingers and toes going numb. The gash on my head hurts, I don't know how much longer until my spine gives out again, and I'm just plain scared.

I see a light up ahead.

Maybe it's help. Maybe I'm already dead and it's heaven. Either way it's not back there and that's all that matters right now. I keep running and running but then my knees constrict, the pain blazing across them in a burning rage. I can't fight this spasm, they give out. I go toppling down in the snow. I try to call out for help but the dizziness and freezing cold takes over. The last thing I see before blacking out are the snowflakes dusting across my lashes, wintery powdered sugar sweetening this absolute hell.

❧ 2 ❧

DERECO

"*But I have a job interview in two days, I can't keep staying here or I'll miss it.*"

Nurse Ann—the she-demon from hell—glares at me over her half- moon spectacles we all suspect she doesn't need and just wears to look smart (which she most definitely is not). "Well—" she taps away on her keyboard, barely paying me any mind. To her I am nothing more than an annoying fly that keeps buzzing around her work space. I am not a person. I am not a being with independent thought; with feelings. "—maybe you should've thought about that before doing something so selfish and stupid."

"Can I please just speak to Dr. Maleks?"

"He's busy."

"How can he be busy when all the patients are out here?"

We're all out here for Reflection Time. I'm supposed to be sitting down and 'reflecting' too. Reflecting on what an awful, selfish, stupid person I am for trying to kill myself. For not thinking about my job interview at Target while my brain was on fire. For not thinking. For caring about my own peace and how there didn't seem to be any other way to find it in that moment.

I wish I was dead now.

Today's suicide plan is to snatch one of the nurses' pencils and stab myself in the jugular so hard and deep that I bleed out. I don't know if I have the nerve though. But with each annoyed sigh and click clack of Nurse Ann's long nails on the keys I get closer and closer to my breaking point.

"If you keep being a problem, I'm going to have to make a note in your file that you're resisting care."

"I'm asking to speak to the doctor. That is the exact opposite of resisting care."

But it's too late. She's opened my file. She's typing the note.

❧

"DAD, HE KEEPS FOLLOWING ME. EVERYWHERE. HE TRIED TO break into

my room last night. I'm scared. Please, please *do something." "I'll talk to them. This is unacceptable. Don't worry."*

❧

"HEARD YOU'RE ON SUICIDE WATCH," JENNY SAYS, FLOPPING down in the chair beside me during Reflection Time. Nurse Ann dramatically shushes her from behind the desk, Jenny flips her off. "What'd you do? Try to hang yourself with a rogue shoelace?"

"No, you ass. I don't even know how to tie a noose."

Jenny laughs. Stanley takes the seat on the other side of me before he *can. Stanley shoots him an intimidating glare and he scurries away. "That's why she's on killer watch, dear Jenny. Her father had the audacity to ask the staff to protect her."*

"Oh Christ." Jenny slumps down in the seat, the cracked fake leather crinkling against her paper pajamas. "Does this guy—" she nods in the direction my stalker has just scurried off in. "—ever take a break from being a fucking perv?"

"No," I say. "Just like Nurse Ratched never takes a break from being a fucking cunt."

Stanley and Jenny laugh. Nurse Ann (Ratched) shushes us again.

Stanley pantomimes being stabbed in the heart. She glares and goes back to furiously typing away, surely adding notes to all our files about what heathen, disgraceful beings we are.

"Should we play sudoku?" Jenny asks.

"Should we stab ourselves with the pencils?" I ask.

Stanley laughs louder, a deep, booming sound that brings me comfort.

"Well they got rid of the ones with erasers so we can rule out consuming those as a form of self-murder."

"What are you three talking about over there?" Nurse Ann screeches.

"Nothing," Jenny shouts back. "Just reflecting on all our sins like good little crazies."

"Don't give me that smart mouth, Jenny. Unless you want another week added to your time."

Jenny scoffs, leans her head on my shoulder. "Bet her paycheck would just love that."

"Do you think they work off commission?" Stanley asks. "Like sales associates in clothing stores. A nice, little bonus per nut job they keep locked up."

"Knowing the way this for profit hell-hole works—" I lean my head on Jenny's. "—probably."

"Do they have you sleeping in the hall now?" Stanley asks me.

My stomach drops. "I don't know. Is that what happens on suicide watch?"

He nods, his eyes pitying. "Afraid so, darling."

"Great. Just great," I huff. "Soon we'll be able to add PTSD from rape to my chart."

"Oh, Jay," Jenny laments. "You've already got it just from being here."

❧

"Good morning, Jay," Tim says cheerily as I sit down beside him for group therapy.

"Morning, Tim."

"Question: is there a giant spider in the middle of the table?" I look to the center of our round table, then back at Tim. I shake my head. He sighs. "What a relief. The new girl, Tracy, said there were bugs in the hall last night."

Tracy has to sleep on a hallway cot now too, The place is overbooked, they've run out of beds. We're like a Days Inn during the holidays.

"Yeah. But we didn't say anything. Because..." I nod to Tim and gesture to the spiderless table. "You know."

Tim taps his nose. "Smart thinking."

"Good morning, my fellow heathens." Stanley drops dramatically into the seat beside Tim. "Did you all see Tracy at breakfast this morning? They confiscated her dimple piercings so she had orange soda coming out her cheeks when I got her laughing."

"Yes, I saw, Stanley," I say with a roll of my eyes. "I was sitting right next to you."

"What was she laughing about?" Tim asks.

"He started singing the matchmaker song from Fiddler on the Roof."

"Why?" Tim says.

"Because that hot, young thing – Andy — just checked in this morning and keeps making eyes at Jay." Stanley does a little shimmy in his seat.

I crumple up a page of my mindfulness workbook and throw it at his head. "You're delusional."

He catches it. "Yes, my dear, we all are."

The rest of our group slowly shuffles in. Stanley, Tim, and I play our daily game of seeing who can spot the most fellow patients trying to sneak in food from breakfast to hoard in their rooms later like *squirrels, and place our bets on who will get away with it. Jenny comes in last and is of course the one to manage such a feat. She smiles like a gold medal olympian when she sits down next to me.*

"Okay, everyone," Melanie, our social worker, and runner up for biggest cunt in the hospital behind Nurse Ann, says. "Today let's start by going around the room and discussing why your behavior hurt the people in your lives and how you can make it up to them when you get out."

"Jokes on her," Jenny whispers in my ear. "We're never getting out."

ONCOMING STORM

I don't know where I am.

The bed beneath me is unfamiliar, the smell of a crackling fire doesn't make sense, and I'm still wearing these god forsaken paper pajamas, albeit they're bloody and torn. Speaking of bloody, my face is no longer caked in it and when I touch my gash I feel a bandage.

I daringly open my eyes.

I'm in a small cabin.

This must be the source of the light I saw.

It's warm and cozy, almost like a hobbit hole. There's a big stone fireplace a few feet from the comfy bed I'm tucked into under a deep green comforter. I can smell peppermint tea wafting from the kitchenette across the room, and see the snow coming down behind the thin, lilac curtains covering the two front windows. I turn my head and almost choke on a scream. There is a gangly, young man standing a few feet from the bed pouring hot water into an old cast iron tub. I gasp. He hears me and looks up.

"Oh, you're awake. Hi."

"Hi," I croak out.

He stands up. He's tall. He has shaggy brown hair that flops in his face, and a gaunt jawline that makes it look like he should be in a Victorian drama set on the city streets of London, not sporting a cable knit sweater and jeans in the middle of the woods. He moves like a loblolly bending in the wind; appearing brittle enough to break but somehow able to weather even the fiercest storm. He must be loblolly strong to be surviving out here on his own—to have carried my limp body through the snow. Which I'm assuming he did, unless the snow fairies have finally come out of my imagination and storybooks to help me in my time of need.

"Did you..." I touch the bandage again to try to process what's happened since I passed out.

"Yeah." The stranger nods, putting his hands in his pockets. "I heard you calling for help. You were only a few yards from the cabin. You were in pretty bad shape when I found you. I used the first aid kit to fix your cut. I'm Laurel, but you can call me Laurie."

"Like in *Little Women*?" I must've hit my head harder than I thought if the first thing I think to ask this stranger is if he's chosen his nickname after a literary character from a Louisa May Alcott novel.

He shrugs. "I haven't read it."

"Do you know what it's about?"

"Women who are little."

"They're not, like, leprechaun little or anything. It's just about the life of these four sisters and Laurie is their next door neighbor."

Laurel nods like this is a normal conversation he's having with an old friend. "Is his full name Laurel too?"

"No, Laurence."

"I don't like the name Laurence."

"Well his first name's Teddy."

"Then why do they call him Laurie?"

I shake my head against the pillow. "Nevermind."

"All right, Jay."

My eyes widen. I sit up too fast, my head spinning. He starts walking over to the bed. Seeing him in fluid motion unsettles me, giving off vibes far too similar to Slenderman and *of course* we're in the middle of the woods.

"How do you know my name?" I try to hide the wavering fear in my voice, but I don't think I'm very successful. The full weight of my situation is sinking in. I'm alone in the woods with a strange, lanky-tree-creepypasta man and I'm wearing clothes made of paper. No one knows where I am and the only people looking for me are cops dispatched by an evil mental hospital.

Tonight is not my night.

Laurie sits on the edge of the bed and sighs. "Relax." He grabs my wrist and holds it up between us, bearing the explanation as to how he knows my name.

My hospital bracelet.

I snatch my wrist away and frantically try to remove it, but it's like these cursed things are made of marble. It's nothing like a cheap paper wristband at a music festival; no matter how I tug and pull I can't get it off. The sound of a switchblade opening pulls my attention back to Laurie. He grabs my wrist, a bit rougher this time, and snaps apart the plastic bracelet with a flick of his knife. He saunters over to the fireplace and tosses the massacred bracelet into the flames. He watches it burn for a few moments, as if he wants to make sure the evidence of my insanity is truly disappearing. Once he seems satisfied, he comes back to the bed.

"It's not what you think," I say.

Laurie smirks. "It is. But that's okay. We're one and the same."

"Um...what?"

He smirks again. He looks too good doing that. It's not

right. An uncanny man alone in the forest shouldn't be so handsome.

"You're not the only crazy running around these woods."

"I'm not crazy."

"What were you in for?" He ignores my insistence on sanity, staring at me with his unblinking, fierce, green eyes. "Let me guess. Suicide attempt."

"I..." I snap my mouth shut. He says it with the same pretentious tone men take when they want to insult girls for ordering pumpkin spice lattes in autumn. "So what? Life sucks, I'm allowed to not want to keep participating."

"Sure. But you seemed pretty desperate not to die earlier. With all that screaming for help."

"I'm also allowed to change my mind."

"Absolutely."

"Well..." I look down at my now bare wrist. It's been months since I've seen it devoid of the revolting, plastic monstrosity. It looks beautiful. "What did *you* go away for?"

"Not suicide." His voice is empty as he says this; his vibrant eyes suddenly seem so dull.

"Did you get released or..."

"I did not get released."

I wrap my fingers around my bare wrist. "What are the odds?"

"That two escaped mental patients would find each other in the middle of the woods during a blizzard? I'm no mathematician, but it does seem pretty unlikely. Maybe we were fated to meet."

I roll my eyes. He chuckles but doesn't say anything else on the matter. "You should bathe while the water's still hot. There's a water pump hooked up to this place that's connected to a well a little ways out back, but it only produces cold water, so if you want a hot bath I suggest doing it now."

I glance at the tub, then back to him.

"I won't look."

To prove his point he gets up and walks to the other side of the room where a small kitchen table sits. He makes a dramatic show of covering his eyes. My body aches, I reek of hospital and sweat. There's dirt and grime in my hair and remnants of dried blood along my jaw. I *need* a bath and now might be my only chance.

I get up, quickly remove my papery excuse for clothes as well as my soaked socks, and practically dive into the tub. The hot water is heaven to my muscles. If this man kills me tonight, at least I'll die without so many spasms imprinted on my spine. I sigh and sink lower in the water, wetting my hair. I hear the sound of Laurie's footsteps, his boots heavy on the old, wooden floor. I sink down deeper into the water to make sure my chest is covered. He rounds the corner of the tub, coming into view, and settles back down on the bed. I watch him from over the lip of the tub, my mouth level with the water.

"Guess you meant you only wouldn't look while I'm getting in."

He makes a show of covering his eyes with his hands.

I laugh.

I can't help it.

Everything's so horrible that something needs to be funny or I'll go insane.

"You don't have to do that." I shift a bit, the water lapping lightly at my skin. "Do you have soap or something I can use?"

Laurie removes his hands, his green eyes glinting in the firelight. "Yep. Wait there."

As if I'd get up.

He returns a few moments later and hands me a bar of soap that smells like eucalyptus and has bits of flower petals molded into it. I get to work scrubbing my battered body with the delectable smelling item.

"It's a body bar," he explains, sitting back on the bed. "You can use it in your hair too."

"Amazing." I smile, lathering up my hands with it. It's so much better than the cheap, chemically smelling stuff at the hospital.

Laurie watches me the whole time with those fire-sharp eyes. I feel tingly under the weight of his gaze, wondering what he went away for. Seeing things that weren't there? Attacking someone? Was he wrongly put away? He's seems insulted by the idea of going away for a suicide attempt but almost everyone I knew in the hospital was there for that. Very few patients were in for delusions or hallucinations.

I think fleetingly of Tim and the bugs. The memory still makes my skin crawl. I shiver beneath the steamy water.

Laurie notices. "Still cold?"

"No. Is this your cabin?"

"I'm fairly confident you can figure out the answer to that yourself."

His voice is saccharine, the tone almost taunting. "Why did you help me?"

Laurie tilts his head like a perplexed dog. Or Michael Meyers after he hung that guy from the kitchen door with a knife.

"Why would I leave you out there to die when I'm right here?"

"You don't know me. You didn't have to save me."

"I don't need to know you to know you're like me enough to deserve saving."

I shake my head slightly, my hair floating in the water; a bathtub Ophelia. "I don't understand."

"Us crazies gotta stick together."

"I'm not—"

"You tried to kill yourself, didn't you?" He smirks again. Bastard.

"You don't understand."

His smirk morphs into a laugh. I want to punch his teeth in. I want to stab a nice stubby pencil into one of the blue veins dancing across his hand.

"Out of everyone out here in the big bad world for miles and miles, I can promise you that I'm the only one who does understand. It's okay to be crazy."

"All right. Fine."

I dunk my head back and let the water wash the soap from my hair. I can feel the hot water quickly cooling around me. The fireplace is fighting to keep the poorly insulated cabin warm but I probably only have a few minutes of good warmth left. I take a deep breath and sink beneath the surface of the water. I open my eyes and watch the strange cabin above me like an oil painting. The colors and lines blend and blur, moving back and forth in a dance. Add a few ballerinas and I'll have my very own Degas masterpiece. I blow bubbles to hold onto my breath a few moments longer. Finally I burst back up into the cold air and crackling firelight, gasping for breath.

"That was a pitiful suicide attempt." Laurie props his elbows on his knees and rests his chin in his hand. *The Thinker*. "And now your bandage is wet."

I touch the mushy excuse for first aid on my head. I rip it away, my irritated skin screaming at me in the process. "It wasn't a suicide attempt. I was savoring the hot water."

"How did you try to do it?"

"You're not very fun to talk to."

Laurie laughs. Leave it to me to end up in the home of the most condescending escaped mental patient ever.

"You think I'm mocking you." His laugh dissipates, his tone disturbingly resolute.

"Because you are. I'm sure some girls find that cute but I just escaped a mental hospital, got into a car crash, and almost froze to death in the woods, so I'm not really up for this type of flirting right now."

Laurie's smirk returns. Like the Cheshire Cat. *We're all mad here.* Fitting.

Maybe I have fallen down a rabbit hole and I'm nowhere near the hospital at all anymore. Safe from the cops and black ice but not from stolen tarts, Caucus Races, and this handsome stranger.

"Your forehead crinkles when you're lost in thought." He stands up and walks over to the sofa where a towel is draped across the back. "I can practically see the ideas racing behind your eyes." He walks back over to me and holds the towel up, closes his eyes.

I stand on shaky legs, my naked body immediately begins to shiver as the now lukewarm water drips down my exposed skin. I grab the towel and wrap it around myself, wishing it would bring me more immediate warmth.

"May I open?"

I discard the ruined bandage in a nearby trash can. "Yeah. Go ahead."

His green eyes greet me once more.

"I laid those clothes out for you. The paper ones you were wearing are bloody and torn."

"Burn them."

He does as I say, adding the hated, pitiful excuse for clothing to the fire that consumed my shackle.

Laurie sits on the couch, lets his head tilt back, and his eyes fall shut. He's giving me privacy again, the only privacy this small space allows. I get out of the tub on shaky legs, and twitching knees. A large plaid button up, a pair of black boxers, and some wool socks have been laid on the bed for me. I get dressed and feel a bit better. Still not warm enough. But better.

"Laurie?" I walk over and stand in front of him.

He opens his eyes and smiles. It's not as taunting this time. "Yes, Jay?"

"Thank you for saving me."

"It was no problem. I've always been good at rescuing broken birds."

I want to take my thank you back.

"I'm not a broken bird."

"Sure you are. Even have the name to match. Jay *Dove*."

He smirks yet again as he recites my full name. I wonder if he committed the rest of my bracelet to memory too. Weight. Eye color.

"That's okay. Don't look so angry." He stands up. His body is suddenly way too close to mine. He smells too good. Like peppermint and the woods. His eyes twinkle as his smile turns mischievous again. "I *like* taking care of broken birds."

The tea kettle screams. Laurie walks over to the kitchenette and takes it off the stove. He grabs two mugs, sprinkles in the peppermint tea leaves I was smelling in the air, and adds the water. He holds a mug out to me. I eye it suspiciously. The bastard laughs.

"You saw me make it." He sips from both mugs dramatically, making a big show of gulping down the scalding liquid. His poor taste buds.

"Fine." I hold my hand out. He walks the mug over to me.

I let it warm my hands and settle back onto the couch. I take a silent moment to appreciate the small mercies of a comfy couch and a warm cup of tea on a wintery night.

"How long have you been out here?" I ask around blowing on my tea.

Laurie sits next to me. Not close enough to make me uncomfortable. I'm grateful for it.

Small mercies. Small mercies.

"About a week or so. Got here right before the snow started. Waiting for it to clear so I can head out."

"How'd you find this place? How did you even get here?"

Laurie quirks one eyebrow up, that stupid smirk sliding across his lips until it fits his mouth perfectly. He sips some of his tea, clearly unaffected by the burning temperature of the liquid.

"I knew a buddy of mine had a cabin out this way and I was delusionally confident that I could find it. Thankfully, my delusions paid off."

"This is your friend's?" I look around the hobbit hole.

He nods. "Yeah. From when I was a kid. They didn't come up here much. Said I could use it if I ever needed a place to get away to."

"That was kind."

Laurie nods his agreement, sips more tea.

"Where are they now?"

"Dead."

The tea is fire in my throat, burning my esophagus. I fight back a cough.

"Don't look like that," Laurie says. "People like us die all the time."

People like us. Crazy people. Sad people. Suicidal people. I wonder what the ratio is of survivors and those who didn't make it through their own attempts; those whose attempts became successes. If you can even stomach calling them that.

"What about *your* friend?" He raises those eyebrows again.

"What friend?"

"Jenny. You called out to her in your sleep a lot. Is she dead too?"

I shift away from him a bit and hope he doesn't notice.

It's disturbing how much he's been able to discern about me in less than a night.

"No." I shake my head, my voice mouse-quiet. "She's still in there. I told her to call me when she gets out. Slipped her my number."

"Risky move."

I nod. It was risky. The staff was constantly telling us that we weren't allowed to share any personal information with each other. No last names, hometowns, nothing. And we certainly weren't allowed to share contact information. They said we'd 'enable' each other if we were to meet up outside of the hospital. Like it was AA or something. Like we were addicted to death.

The staff are idiots. Cruel, vindictive idiots.

We *need* each other inside and outside. We are the only ones who can understand not only the trauma of surviving a suicide attempt but also the horrors of what happens behind closed doors in the mental health field. No one really knows unless they endure it. And so few believe it. They all figure us crazies must be over exaggerating. I need Jenny and Stanley so badly and I'm so terrified I won't ever see them again. My chest aches with the pain of missing them already and it hasn't even been a full twenty-four hours yet.

"Strange, isn't it?" Laurie asks.

"What?"

"Wanting to live so badly. Wanting to escape the place they put you in to keep you alive. To protect you from yourself."

A cold, hollow laugh bubbles up in my mouth. I shake my head, let my eyes settle on the fire. "They don't protect us. They just kill us more slowly than we were killing ourselves."

"I know. But you must want to live if you left. If you ran into the woods the way you did just to get away from them."

I unfocus my gaze so the fire becomes a beautiful, blurry,

Monet-like image in front of me. "Yeah. It's like...I realized I didn't want to go the second I leaned over the edge." I bite my lip, Laurie keeps watching me. Clearing for the clock in my mind to tick its conclusion. "It's not that I wanted to *actually* die, I wanted someone to beg me to live. To prove to me that I'm not this unloveable, burdensome waste of space. Not just regurgitate all that 'it gets better' bullshit, but rather give me a clear cut plan on how it can and will get better. How my life could be something bearable again. And instead I got sent somewhere that made me wish I'd succeeded in falling."

"So you were a jumper?" I tear my gaze away from the fire and look into his burning green eyes. I nod. "Classic." He clinks his tea mug against mine.

"You didn't go away for suicide." He nods. "But did you ever want to?"

"Kill myself?"

"Yes."

"Of course. Almost did one time. But my sister stopped me."

"What were you doing?"

He drinks more tea. "It's a pretty gory tale for a sweet girl like you."

I huff another laugh. He smiles and I can't see the sky from this far down the rabbit hole.

"Was going to stab myself in the gut. She wrestled the knife away from me. Held me all night on the kitchen floor as I sobbed."

"I think...if my sister had been there she would've helped me differently. At least I like to think that."

"Who sent you to the nut house then?"

"My parents. They thought it was the right thing to do."

"Most usually do."

I slide down further on the couch, the tea swishing in the

mug as I rest it on my stomach, the warmth comforting me as it radiates across my chilled skin.

"I can't go back," I whisper to the fire.

I feel Laurie's hand on my shoulder. It's a gentle touch. Light yet firm enough to comfort. I slowly turn my gaze back to him. His eyes are so captivating I could get consumed by them (would I even mind if I was?), a teacake slipping away as it's soaked in caramel.

He gives my shoulder a soft squeeze.

"You won't. I'll make sure of it."

"Why? Why are you helping me so much?"

He drops his hand. "I told you, us crazies gotta stick together."

✿ 4 ✿
HOOK ECHO

They've turned off the water. Said it was because there's something wrong with the plumbing, the workers will be here soon, it won't be all day. None of us believe them, about any of it. I desperately need to change my tampon but they won't even let us in the bathroom. No one drinks anything at breakfast or lunch, terrified of wetting ourselves—something we'll surely be punished for. My tongue is desert dry, my eyes water, my knees scream. It's been several days since I've had anything to drink besides soda. The dehydration ravages my inflamed muscles. It might kill me soon.

"Every time you think this shithole can't get worse," Stanley mutters, slouching down into the seat beside me.

Waterfall noises blare from the old stereo across the room. I imagine myself smashing it into a million pieces. Taking a particularly jagged one and slicing my throat. If the water really is off, then there will be no way to wash away the mess.

"Did you hear we're going to start getting new worksheets?" Jenny joins us.

"What kind of worksheets?" I ask.

"Tracy said they had them at the last joint she was in. You get *them in the morning before breakfast. We have to write down if we feel homicidal or suicidal and rank the feeling on a scale of 1 to 10 then at the end of the day before bed we go over if the numbers have changed."*

The three of us burst out laughing at the absurdity of such a thing.

Most of us feel both desires at a full blown ten everyday, there's no way any of us are going to tell the truth. I may want to die, but I don't want to die here. *It's the only thing keeping me going.*

"I was talking to my mom last night," I say. "She asked me if the nature trails were nice."

"Nature trails?" They both look perplexed.

I nod. "Apparently the website says there's lots of nature trails we get to walk every day during—" I wave my hand around the bleak room. "—reflection time."

There's a pause.

We all begin to laugh again.

None of us have seen the sun in weeks.

❧

"WAKE UP." TRACY NUDGES ME FROM THE COT NEXT TO MINE. Both of us are crowded into the hall with the other overflow patients and suicide watchers (like me). "They're playing Criminal Minds.*" She points to the tiny TV mounted on the wall.*

I groan as I sit up. It's the first time the TV has played anything but the Weather Channel.

Tracy puts a finger to her lips. I smile and nod. If we draw attention to the show that some clueless nurse must've switched on without realizing, then we'll lose TV privileges and be forced to stare at the wall for entertainment.

Or play more sudoku.

Without erasers.

Life is hell.
And they wonder why we all want to die.

PUTTING ME IN A COT IN THE HALLWAY DIDN'T STOP HIM.

5

THE EYE OF THE STORM

My sleep is as paper thin as the hospital pajamas. It's because of this that the sound of heavy foot-steps in the snow wakes me. I sit up, slick with sweat despite the cold. The fire is doing its best to keep the cabin warm but the night is viscous—the sharp air seeping through every fissure and crack. I hold my breath and listen closely. I can definitely hear footsteps nearing the cabin, accompanied by a pair of men's voices.

I get out of bed and softly pad across the floor to where Laurie is asleep on the sofa under a pile of old quilts. I kneel down beside him, shaking his shoulder. "Laurie. Laurie, wake up."

He opens his eyes, groggy with the haze of freshly disturbed sleep. "What's wrong?"

"I heard someone outside."

He shifts a bit, clearly still not fully in the waking world. "Sometimes I think I hear people outside too, but the forest just makes scary sounds at night. It's worse when you're alone. Go back to sleep and—"

I grip his arm firmly, my fingers digging in against his sweater.

"*No.* Listen. Can't you hear it, too?"

Laurie sits up, not bothering to remove my hand's hold on him. I don't dare let go. I'm terrified and he's my only anchor in this savage sea of snow and startling sounds. I watch his eyes as he goes still and listens to the night. I see them flash, a sign he's heard it too.

"Someone's coming," I insist.

"You're right. Quick, put the fire out."

I get up and race across to the kitchen. I grab the tea kettle that now contains chilled water, rush back, and douse the fire. Laurie shifts around me and grabs something from beside the fireplace. It's not until he's standing by the barred door that I realize what it is.

An ax.

The kind for chopping firewood.

It makes my stomach sick. I clench my hands into fists at my side, try to steady my breathing. Laurie meets my stare across the dark. His eyes seem to say it's okay, he's not going to use the ax, it's just in case whoever is on the other side of that door is violent. Unsure of what I'm meant to do, I creep over to stand beside him. He holds out a hand for me and I take it, our chilled palms encasing each other like a bullet in a shell.

The voices and footsteps are coming up the front porch steps. I hold my breath.

A fist bangs on the door.

"Hello?" the voice calls out. "Anyone home? It's the police." My eyes go wide. I tug on Laurie's hand. He looks back at me but I don't understand the message in his eyes anymore. "We saw a light in the window just a moment ago." The cop sounds like he's faking politeness. "We know someone's home. Why don't you open up? We'd just like a word with you about a missing person reported in the area. Maybe you've seen her."

Laurie drags me back towards the sofa. "Stay here," he whispers. "Be quiet, be still."

"It's me." Tears well in my eyes, fire burns in my chest, panic rips through my heart. "They're looking for me."

"I know. I won't let them take you. Trust me. Please."

Tea and some shared experiences by a warm fire is not nearly enough to entrust my safety to a woodland stranger wielding an ax. But it's between him, the cops, and the cold.

I choose him.

"Okay," I breathe.

He gives my hand a squeeze then drops it.

"Hold on a minute," he calls out to the cops, making his voice sound as groggy as it did a few minutes ago. "I was asleep." He shuffles loudly over to the door, groaning as he does, making a show of it all. Maybe he was an actor before his life became defined by illness and hospitalization. "I haven't seen any girl." He stands close to the door but makes no move to open it.

"How about you open up and we have a chat?" The second voice says. Another cop.

"Sorry, officers. Unless you've got a warrant, I'm not opening the door. It's the middle of the night in the middle of a blizzard. I'd be a damn fool to open the door to two strangers just cause you claim to be cops looking for some damsel in distress."

"Sir," the first cop's false polite tone has vanished, "this woman isn't any damsel. She's an escaped mental patient."

"I wasn't aware there was a criminal insane asylum around here." Laurie's voice is lilting with sarcasm. It's a marvel to watch.

"There isn't. Just a regular one."

"Then why should I be worried? If she's not a violent criminal then—"

"Sir!" The cop sounds furious now. "Open the door. We have reason to believe that she's here."

"Well that's just silly," Laurie says. "I'm all alone. Have been for ages now."

"We found the car she stole crashed on the side of the road," the second cop chimes in, a little less forcefully than the first. "This cabin is the only thing for miles. We would've found a body if she didn't make it."

"Open the door," the first cop seethes.

Laurie glances at me and sighs. The panic explodes in my chest; an atomic bomb radiating through my bloodstream. How can I have fought so hard to get out just to be given up so easily?

"Laurie," I whisper. "Please—"

"You really don't want me to open this door, officers."

The rest of my sentence gets lodged in my throat. What is he doing? He meets my gaze and winks, his grin dazzling even in the dark.

"Don't worry, little bird."

"Open the damn door!" The first cop bangs his fist on the door.

"Well." Laurie shrugs. "I did warn you."

He lifts the bar, opens the door and before the first cop can say a single word, Laurie raises the ax and brings it down on the man's head. My hands fly to cover my mouth, stifling my own scream as I watch the stranger's eyes roll back in his head and blood gushes across his skull, staining his skin as it rivulets down his face. He makes a sickening gurgling sound and falls face first onto the porch. The second cop stands stunned behind him. Laurie grins wickedly, blood splattered across his face, like he's a walking, talking Jackson Pollock painting. The second cop fumbles for his gun but the shock has turned his fingers to butter. He isn't quick enough. He should've had the weapon trained on the door from the start if he wanted to survive this. Laurie lunges forward, this time I *do* scream. I step forward towards the doorway but stop myself when I see the ax make contact with the side of the second cop's head. The sound of the blade hitting skin and bone makes my stomach churn and bile burn in the back of my throat. Laurie laughs as more blood paints the porch.

Like the Mad Hatter spilling a cup of tea.

The cop's mouth falls open in a silent plea. I step a bit closer to the doorway, unable to look away from the massacre in front of me. The dying man's eyes find mine.

"You," he whispers.

"Her," Laurie taunts.

My savior—this brutal monster—yanks the ax free of the man's skull and brings it back again, hacking into his neck, slicing his throat down to the bone. My knees give up and I choke on the vomit in my throat. I drop my gaze to the floor as I hear the loud thump of the cop hitting the porch. It's followed by the familiar sound of Laurie's footsteps. I bring my gaze back up and almost scream again. Laurie stands in the doorway, covered in blood, the ax dripping blood by his side.

"It's okay." His voice is back to normal. "You're safe now." My eyes go to the ax.

He notices.

Laurie walks into the cabin. I quickly get to my feet and stumble backwards, head spinning, spine spasming. He stops a few feet from me. The dim moonlight streams through the open doorway, casting shadows across the blood on his face. I watch as he sets the ax down by the door and moves even closer to me, arms out like he's approaching a skittish animal.

"Jay, it's alright. I'm not going to hurt you."

I have no words, nothing makes sense now. The small

scrap of safety I found tonight has been irrevocably shattered —*gutted.*

"Please don't look at me like that. What else was I supposed to do?"

"I don't know," I whisper. "You could've let them take me."

"No." His voice is fervent. Determined. "I told you I'd protect you."

"Okay." I choke on the sob crawling up my throat. "Okay."

I can tell he's not sure if he believes me. But I just have to appear calm until he's gone. As soon as he's not looking I'll take my coat and boots and run. If I can make it back to the road, I can walk until I reach a town. If I get really desperate, I can resort to hitchhiking. A stranger on the road can't be any more dangerous than the stranger before me.

"I have to get rid of the bodies." He says this so cavalierly, like he's just commenting on needing to take out the trash or change the sheets or turn over the laundry. Not dispose of human bodies. "Can you wait here? Just stay here, all right?"

I nod, practically gagging on the bile clogging my throat. "All right."

He nods. I remain perfectly still despite the pain and watch him leave. I continue to stay still as I listen to him drag a body away. I rush to the window and peek around the curtains. The body of the second cop is still on the porch. A trail of crimson leads through the snow, into the thick of the woods. I have no idea how long it's going to take him to do whatever it is he plans on doing but I don't have any intention of being here when he comes back for the second body. I move as fast as my shaky legs and spasming spine will allow. I stuff my feet into my laceless boots and pull on Stanley's coat. I wish I had money or a phone or even just a hat. The wind whistles outside, the snow coming down even harder than before.

Just get to the road.

There's one thing I can take with me.

I run to the kitchenette and begin pulling open cabinets and drawers, finding the place surprisingly well stocked.

At last I locate a knife.

❧

IT ONLY TAKES ME TEN MINUTES IN THE STORM TO GET turned around. Hopelessly lost.

The tears freeze as soon as I shed them, the sharp icy sensation

burning my cheeks. My ears and nose turn cherry red as the wind whips my skin raw. My knees twitch sharply with every step, the snow too deep, my boots too useless. Stanley's coat feels like it weighs a hundred pounds, my inflamed shoulders struggle to stand straight under the mass of it. But I can't stop. If I stop, I'll freeze to death.

I am not dying here.

I wonder what time it is. It must be well after midnight by now. Maybe it will be easier to find the road in the morning. If I can keep walking until dawn, keep the blood flowing then maybe—

I hear a rustle.

A crunch in the snow.

"Jay!"

No.

I grip the knife hilt tight and try to run. The boots are weighing me down. I'm going to twist my ankle if I keep trying to make it with these stupid things on. I can hear Laurie getting closer and closer. The shadows and snow will only keep me hidden for a few more moments if I don't do something fast.

I kick off the boots, the wool socks Laurie gave me sinking into the freezing snow. I cry out without thinking, the cold is needles against the soles of my feet, the material is soaked through within seconds.

Go. Go. Go.

"Jay, this is stupid. Come back."

I turn towards the sound of his voice. He's so close. With my feet free of the burden of the boots, I take off running again. My toes are quickly going numb, my lips are so chapped I'm sure they'll crack and bleed soon, and my bones hurt. I duck behind a big tree, press my back against the trunk and try to catch my breath. I can hear Laurie's loud footsteps relentlessly crunch, crunch, crunching in the snow.

"Jayyyyy." His voice has turned disturbingly sing-song. "Come out, come out wherever you are."

I close my eyes, more painful tears slide down my cheeks. He's insane. I was wrong. This isn't *Alice's Adventures in Wonderland,* it's *American Psycho.*

"No point in hiding from me." He's so close now. I can see his shadow moving across the snow. "I'm going to find you, so you may as well save us both the trouble and stop this now."

I slide a hand into the pocket of Stanley's coat, touching the piece of paper, begging it to give me some semblance of strength. It crinkles beneath my touch, tells me to keep going. I steel myself against the agonizing cold and take off running. The tree branches reach for me like monstrous hands in the dark. One scrapes my face, cutting deep. I hiss sharply, wet blood trickles through my frozen tears.

"Jay! Goddammit!" His footsteps turn to running. The crunching is louder and louder in my ears. I bite my tongue to keep from sobbing.

My socks are soaked through, my chest is burning. Stanley's coat is so heavy. My bones rattle beneath my skin, my muscles blaze with inflammation, my eyes itch from the icy tears. But I can't stop. Then my lower back spasms so severely I scream and fall forward, my knees and hands slamming down into the snow. I have to fight. It's the only choice now. I get back up, standing on my pitiful, shaky legs, brandishing the knife in front of me. Laurie breaks through the thicket of trees in front of me, remnants of blood still spattered across his cheeks and the bridge of his nose, my discarded boots hanging from his spindly fingers. His green eyes glow in the starlight—the sight is almost otherworldly. He looks at the knife then looks into my eyes.

"Jay, put that down."

My hand shakes. "Stay away from me."

"I'm not going to hurt you. Come back to the cabin. You can't stay out here. We're in the eye of the storm."

That's putting it lightly.

The world spins around me. I wish I had done a dozen things differently when escaping the hospital. I wish I could go way back and never get up on that roof. I should've just swallowed my sadness and endured it. What I felt then is still present but now I have new horrors added to the mix. It's suffocating. It's deadly. Dying by my own hand seemed noble somehow. Brave. Dying alone in the woods at the hands of a psychotic man feels like a cheap joke. I'm going to become a statistic and not the kind that gets true crime podcasts. No one's going to care about the disabled mental patient that went missing in the middle of a blizzard. No one's ever going to know that I tried to live.

I'm trying.

I won't stop trying. Not after everything. I won't make it easy for him.

"Jay, please. If you stay out here you'll die."

"And if I go with you I won't?"

"Why would I kill you?"

"I don't know! You're clearly insane!"

"So are you."

I shake my head and take a step back. He takes a step forward.

"I'm not."

"You are. And that's okay."

"Fuck you!" I turn to run but my body chooses this exact moment to send a blinding stream of pain throughout my entire spine. I shriek and collapse to my knees, the knife falling from my grip as my body convulses.

"Well, well, well." I hear Laurie march over to me, tilting his head as he takes in the sight of me. "If it isn't a little, broken bird."

I make a sound akin to a growl, standing again on staggering feet, my eyelids fluttering as I fight the oncoming blackout. My body burns so badly I can't tell where the pain ends and I begin. The forest tilts again. Wonderland is nightmarish now.

You're late, Alice.

I'm too late. I'm going to die alone in the middle of the woods. The snow will bury my body. Soon I'll be nothing but a collection of wintery bones.

"Jay, you're hurt. Stop this."

"Stay away." I try to sound strong but my voice shakes.

I try to run again but Laurie's too quick for my battered body.

He chases after me, tackling me to the ground. I scream and flail. I try to aim for his groin, his eyes, his nose—anything. But despite his gangly frame, he's too strong. He grabs my wrists in his hand and pins them down above my head, his thighs bracketing me in, pressing me down into the snow. I scream and writhe but it's no use. He's got me.

"Jay! Stop it!"

I openly sob. I can't help it. "Please," I gasp. "Just let me go. I won't tell anyone."

He grunts in annoyance. "Fucking hell. You're hysterical. I killed those cops to protect you. I won't hurt you."

I close my eyes, I can't bear the burn of his green-eyed gaze. "I don't believe you," I whisper.

"I know you don't. But it's the truth. I didn't save you just to

kill you."

I open my eyes and am taken aback by the look in his gaze. It seems almost forlorn.

"But I'm not allowed to leave."

"If there wasn't a fucking blizzard I would escort you back to the road myself. But if the choices are between forcing you to stay with me or standing back and letting you wander into the woods towards your death, then I'm going to choose the former. Even if it makes you hate me."

"I wasn't wandering towards my death."

"You're not wearing shoes or pants and the road is in the opposite direction. And there's clearly something wrong with you, you keep falling."

I clench my jaw. I know my disability is showing more than it has in ages but I still hate it being seen, especially now, especially by him. "I'm fine."

"You're not. You're injured."

"I'm not. I'm just like this."

"Unable to walk or stand for long periods of time?"
"Please get off me." I close my eyes again.

"Do you promise not to run away if I do?"

"Do you promise not to hurt me?"

Laurie sighs again. This time it doesn't sound frustrated, it sounds depleted. Like he's as beaten down as I feel. I feel his forehead lightly brush against mine and his hot breath ghost across my neck. I twitch against the dueling sensations.

They're so light, so faint, yet they wash over me like a tidal wave.

"I promise I won't hurt you. Now please come back to the cabin and let me take care of you."

I shouldn't trust him. It's incredibly stupid to trust him. But if I don't, I'm going to die out here. I guess it's the devil you know and all that. I open my eyes to see that he has his closed, his forehead grazing mine. He's breathing slowly. I can smell the blood on him, mixed in with the woodsy scent of the fireplace and the sweetness of the peppermint tea, still fresh on his breath even after hours of sleep.

"Okay," I whisper.

Laurie opens his eyes. "All right. Come on."

He gets off of me and holds his hands out. I let him pull me up to stand, my body still wailing in pain. I watch as he analyzes my obvious state of distress. "Come on, little bird." He hoists me onto his back and begins to carry me to the cabin. The blood and bodies are gone and a fire is burning in the hearth again. He tosses my pitiful boots aside, then settles me down on the couch and goes to lock and bar the door.

"Laurie."

He walks back from the door to stand before me. I look up at him and feel my stomach churn. In the blazing firelight his grisly appearance is far more vibrant than before.

"What is it?" he asks.

"Can you...um...wash your face?" "Sure."

He heads to the bathroom. I shift anxiously on the couch. I remove my soaked socks and drape Stanley's coat across the back of the sofa. I grab one of the blankets Laurie was using and pull it around my shoulders. I can't stop shaking. From the cold. From the shock. Laurie returns a few minutes later sporting a clean face and a new sweater and carrying a first aid kit. There's no trace of his violent acts left on his body. I take in the sight of him. He looks so harmless like this. So sweet.

Laurie kneels before me and opens the first aid kit. He takes out a bottle of hydrogen peroxide and a cotton ball. He wets the cotton ball and holds it up to my face. "May I?" I nod. "It'll sting a bit."

"I know how it works," I snap.

His sneaky smirk returns. "All right then."

He presses the cotton ball against the gash in my cheek. It *does* sting. I clench my jaw to keep from hissing. He cleans the cut methodically, his eyes never wavering. "So do you want to explain to me now why you kept collapsing?" he asks.

I shift under the blanket. Anxious against his gaze. "It's not a big deal. I have degenerative disc disease and fibromyalgia."

"That sounds like a big deal if it affects your mobility so much at such a young age."

"I'm twenty-three."

He smiles. "That's young."

"You look the same age as me."

He takes a tube of ointment out of the kit and spreads some

across my cut. "Twenty-one."

Great. I'm trapped with a mad man who's barely old enough

to drink.

"I usually have a cane. But...they took it. Said it could too easily be used as a weapon."

"So you've just been struggling to move easily since you got put in the hospital?" His voice drips with disgust. I nod. He puts a bandage across my cheek then moves to apply more ointment to my car crash induced forehead gash. "How long were you there?"

"Eight months. I think. It got hard to keep track of time."

"Fucking bastards." He looks terrifying again, it's staggering how quickly his features can morph into something monstrous. He notices my discomfort. Of course he does. He sets the ointment aside, reaching for another bandage. "Please don't look at me like that." He applies the second bandage gently to my forehead, mending the last of my wounds.

"I can't help it. You're a killer."

"I know. But it's not like I went looking for it. If I didn't, then they would've taken you back and I couldn't let that happen."

"Why not? You don't even know me. You just met me tonight."

"Because—" he rests his hands on my knees. I don't know why, but I feel my muscles relax against his touch. "—I don't need to know you for ages to know that a sweet girl like you doesn't deserve to be in a place like that."

I look down at his hands. His fingers are long and lithe, the veins under his skin a collection of dancing indigos and azuls. They look like lovely hands to be held by. To be touched by. It's almost impossible to believe that just an hour ago they wielded a murder weapon.

"What about you, Laurie? Do you deserve to be in a place like that?"

Laurie squeezes my knees. I meet his gaze.

"I wasn't in a place like the one you were in."

My chest tightens again. My head spins. I suspected it as soon as I woke up here. I suspected it when he picked up the ax.

I suspected it as he carried me back through the blizzard. It's so obvious but I didn't want to acknowledge it. Didn't want to accept it. I still don't. But I can't ignore it anymore. Not after what I've seen him do.

"You were in a hospital for the criminally insane," I say softly. "Weren't you?"

"Yes, I was."

"Did you kill someone?"

"Yes."

He says it so simply. So matter of fact. There's no joy in the confession but it sickens me nonetheless. "Who?"

"It doesn't matter. Just trust that I'm not some monster. Trust that I can take care of you."

"I can't. I don't know you." *And you're a killer.*

"You do. And I know you. Time doesn't always matter so much."

I shake my head and pull my legs up under me, tucking them beneath the blanket. I want to just cocoon myself in and pretend this day never happened, pretend the last eight months never happened. I let my head fall forward and rest on my blanketed knees, the soft fabric of the quilt blocking out Laurie's green- eyed gaze.

"Once the storm clears, I can help you get to town."

I hear him shifting. I turn my head to the side, my cheek cradled against the blanket's surface to see Laurie has stood up, looking down at me—a tree blowing in the wintry wind. I almost laugh at the idea of this lanky creature being the one to guide me through the snow and wilderness back to the road. He looks like the slightest gust would send him crashing to the ground. His strength is a secluded secret he keeps hidden behind his knobby knees and sharp elbows.

"Laurie."

"Jay."

"You've been here for more than a week, haven't you?"

He puts his hands in his pockets. "Why do you think that?" "The kitchen is full of food and supplies. And not things that someone who hasn't been here in years would have waiting." Laurie stares at me, his jaw stony and still, his eyes grim and unblinking.

"I assume there's a town close by where you've been getting groceries and the like."

"Yes." He nods once. "There is."

"And you drove here? In a car I'm guessing can't weather the snow or you'd help yourself be rid of me already."

"I'm not trying to be rid of you. I have nothing against you,

Jay."

No, just against the men you've killed.

He sighs. "I'd like to go back to sleep. There's no point arguing about this in the middle of the night."

He nods to the bed, clearly wanting for me to return to it and leave him alone. I oblige and de-blanket my feet to shuffle over to the bed. I crawl into its blessed warmth, letting the silence of the cabin settle over me as Laurie begins to rebuild the fire until the familiar crackling fills the empty space.

"You can sleep with the knife if it'll make you feel better."

"It's fine," I grumble. I'd never be able to overpower him anyway.

"Okay, goodnight, Jay." "Goodnight, Laurie."

❦

I WAKE TO THE SMELL OF CHOCOLATE CHIP PANCAKES. THE snow is still coming down outside beneath the shadows of a cloudy, sunny sky. Laurie is in the kitchenette, flipping pancakes on a griddle, sporting a 'Kiss the Cook' apron. His hair flops in his eyes when he looks over to smile at me.

"Morning, roomie."

I roll my eyes. I feel like I'm back in a demented version of college. I wonder which roommate I hate more, the bitch I shared a dorm with freshman year, the patient in the hospital who spread feces on the walls of our room, or him, the ax murderer. It's a tough call. But the other two didn't make chocolate chip pancakes.

"I made some tea." He points to the small table where two mugs are laid out. "It's chai, black tea. Caffeine helps with pain, right?"

I nod, feeling numb. "Yes." My voice is soft and scratchy from sleep. "I don't suppose you have any ibuprofen in this place?"

"I think there's some in the bathroom. There's also some jars of willow bark in here, you could chew on one."

"Why is there willow bark in there?"

"For willow bark tea."

"Are you, like, big into tea?"

He sports a look of pure joy. "Oh yeah. Worked in a tea shop all throughout high school. Kind of an expert by now and out here in the wilderness you can find lots of fresh ingredients. Not so much now that the ground's frozen though." He shrugs and returns his attention to the pancakes.

Of course he's a tea sommelier, it's weirdly specific and doesn't match him as he's presented himself at all which in a way is entirely on brand for what little I know about him so far.

The Mad Hatter invites Alice to tea.

Who am I to refuse? I'm so hungry and I can't remember the last time I had something caffeinated. Caffeine isn't allowed in the hospital, it's contraband. They're convinced it will ignite some kind of rage in us. Or, God forbid, *joy*. Can't let the crazies have control over their emotions, now can we?

I get up and make my way slowly to the bathroom, my bare feet flinching against the floor. I miss my borrowed socks. It takes some scouring but I locate a tiny travel bottle of Advil with three lone pills at the bottom. I hold my hand under the icy tap for some of the well water, use it to choke down all three pills in one go. Back in the kitchenette Laurie is plating several pancakes for me. I sit down opposite him, staring at the breakfast food, unsure of what to do.

"You okay?" he asks.

"Not at all."

He barks out a laugh. "Yeah, I wouldn't think so. But you will be."

I drown my sugary sustenance in syrup, Laurie does the same and we eat in silence for several painful minutes.

"How long do you think until the storm lets up?" I finally ask.

"Another day? Two at most. I'm not an expert or anything, but these blizzards rarely last more than a handful of days."

I lean back in the chair and nod, chewing on a big bite of pancakes. They're so good. Damn him. "And then we can try and get to town? I can call my sister. I guess I could call her from here. Is it shooting for the stars to hope you have a phone?"

"I have one of those cheap burner ones. It just makes calls.

Service is terrible out here, but you're welcome to try."

He gets up and moves across the room to the shelf over the mantle. How did I not notice it sitting there last night? He brings the phone back over to me.

"Why didn't you ask me last night if I needed to make a call?"

"It was kind of late by the time you woke up. And after that...well..."

I take the phone from his chilly fingertips. "Yeah," I mumble.

I click the phone's power button. There's not even one measly bar. I set it down on the table as he sits back down across from me.

"No good?"

I shake my head. "I guess it would be ridiculous to call her from here anyway. It's not like she can get to us or us to her in the middle of all this." I wave a hand to the windows where the snow is covered in the curtains' lavender hazy light.

"You'll be able to call her from town. The days will pass by quickly."

He's trying to make me feel better. It's jarring.

My spine clenches as a burning spasm travels through the tendons. I clench my teeth until my jaw aches, my eyes closing as I try to envision a glowing white light to block out the pain, or at least quell the agony. That's what my old meditation app told me to do. It's never worked for more than a few seconds at most but I don't know what else to do.

"Jay? What's wrong?"

"Nothing."

I gasp, my eyes shooting open. Laurie's cold hand is resting on top of mine, his long arm stretched out across the table. "Are you in pain?"

"I—" tears suddenly well in my eyes without warning, a sob catches in my chest. Without thinking I let my head fall forward until it meets the tabletop with a thud. I wish I had my mom or sister here to help me, their attempts at healing massage exacted with clumsy fingers brought a comfort I've been devoid of for months. The pain manifests past the physical until I feel it in my heart, in my soul. I'm so lonely and unhappy and in so much fucking pain; every shade, every hue, it coats me, it drowns me.

"How can I help?"

Laurie's voice is so soft I'm amazed I'm able to hear him over the riot of misery happening inside my mind. I lift my head as much as I can without causing the tendons in my neck to burn.

"What?" I must have misheard him.

"You're collapsed on my table in pain, how do I help you?"

"You don't, it'll pass. Eventually."

"I could..." he meets my gaze, his eyes asking the silent question.

Am I willing to let him touch me? Am I willing to give my battered body over to his hands, put trust in the pressure of his fingers and knuckles, have faith that he won't hurt me the way he's hurt others? But those long fingers, those strong hands could probably knead out the menacing knots in my muscles and soothe the gunky, burning adhesions in my arms. I sniffle, blinking back tears and nod.

"Yeah, just—" I manage to sit up and press my fingers to where the pain starts at the base of my skull. "—here is where it starts." Laurie gets up and moves behind me.

The pressure from his hands is light at first but slowly morphs into a beautiful impact as he deftly teases away the fiery spasms and locked trigger points from my muscles, massaging my discs into a calmer state of being. He slides his fingers up into my hair and begins to massage my scalp. The feeling is heavenly. I always forget how the pain can radiate into my skull. I groan softly when a particularly nasty knot above my left ear finally releases, the trigger point sending a warm sensation all the way down to my toes. Nearly half an hour later my body feels more bearable than it has in a long, long time.

"Sorry, my hands are cramping." Laurie retracts his fingers. "Just give me a minute to—"

"No." I turn around, looking up at him. "You don't need to do any more, that was a big help. Really. Thank you."

The corner of his mouth lifts up in a half smile.

"Let me reheat the tea. Chew on the bark. It'll help."

I do as he says, nibbling away at the bark, watching as his body swishes around the kitchen to heat more water for the tea. He moves like life's a ballet and he's the principal dancer putting on the most elegant show. Once he finishes and sets his sights back on me, I can see a nervousness in him that unmoors me. It's as if he's the one who's scared. Afraid of me and my banshee screeches and spasming spine.

"I need to go chop some more firewood," he says. "It's best to do it while the sun's still high in the sky."

I nod like I know anything about how living in the woods works.

Then I remember what he'll need to chop firewood.

"Don't worry," he says, clearly registering my alarm. "I put the ax outside and I'll leave it out there when I'm done."

"Great, now I feel so comforted." My tone is droll and sarcastic. You would almost think I'm joking.

Laurie laughs like I am.

I smile. He's hard to stay mad at.

Laurie bundles up in a coat, hat, and scarf, tugs on some big boots and heads out. Leaving me alone in the hobbit hole. I have no idea how long he'll be gone. How long does chopping firewood take? Twenty minutes? An hour? It can't be a speedy process, surely. I get up and begin to wander the tiny space in search of anything to occupy my mind. There isn't much. A rogue comic book on the kitchen counter, some superhero I'm not familiar with, a yoyo on the mantle, the kind that glows in the dark. I pick it up and give it a go, watching as it bounces up and down a few times, Kate Bush lyrics echoing in my head as I do. *You're like my yoyo that glowed in the dark. What made it special, made it dangerous.* I put the yoyo back and continue my hunt for something to hold my attention. Salvation comes in the form of a worn cardboard box tucked away under the bed that's full of dusty books with water stained pages. All classics. All paperback and crinkly and beautifully old. They must belong to Laurie's friend. I sort through them and settle on *The Secret Garden.*

I open the small chest of drawers by the bed, retrieve a

pair of Laurie's jeans and slip them on. I have to roll the waistband several times and severely cuff the legs. I also locate some more warm socks to save my poor, chilly toes. The quilt on the couch welcome's me as I re-cocoon myself in its warmth. I open the book, mindful of its fragile cover.

When Mary Lennox was sent to Misselthwaite Manor to live with her uncle, everybody said she was the most disagreeable-looking child ever seen.

The familiar first sentence brings me a small semblance of peace. I easily get lost in the story, the time swiftly ticking by with the flipping of pages. A hundred pages later I'm pulled from the story by the sound of Laurie's boots stomping off excess snow on the front porch. He enters the cabin, rosy-cheeked, arms full of freshly chopped firewood.

"Hey," he pants, his breath still frosty as it becomes dragon smoke in the air. I watch as his gangly figure makes its way to the hearth and deposits the wood by its side. He prods the fire a few times with the poker then adds another log. "Want lunch?" "We had breakfast not that long ago."

He shrugs. "Let's make a snack then." He returns to the kitchenette and starts to arrange the ingredients for cookies. "Come join me, Jay."

"Every meal we have can't consist of chocolate chips." I set the book aside and make my way over.

He smirks, takes the ridiculous 'Kiss the Cook' apron off its hook on the wall and presents it to me like he's knighting me.

"Of course it can, little bird."

I fasten the apron strings behind my back, rolling my eyes.

"Stop calling me that. It's demeaning."

"Birdy?"

"Jay," I insist.

"Jay is a type of bird. So why not Birdy?"

"No. You don't see me trying to saddle you with dumb nicknames."

"You could." He starts adding ingredients to a large bowl without even bothering to measure them. He must do this often. "Why are you so grumpy? Pain?"

Little does he know, I'm always grumpy.

"I'm constantly in pain. I idle at five on the scale doctors give. You know, the one with the smiley faces that progressively get angrier."

"What does the smiley face look like at five?" he asks.

I point to my face, my expression apathetic; unamused. He laughs, the sound seeming to rattle his slender bones. "If you're in too much pain to help bake, you can just keep me company."

"This place is one room. I don't have much of a choice."

He shoots me a smirk drenched in quirked eyebrows. I sigh, dramatically collapsing down into one of the kitchen chairs.

"So, Jay, tell me a story." He begins a thorough mixing process. "A story?"

He nods. Mixes. Mixes.

"Okay." I rack my brain for anything compelling to say. I end up settling on his namesake. "Want to hear the story of *Little Women?*"

He looks up from the batter, green eyes glimmering. "The women who are little but not leprechaun little? Absolutely, Birdy. Take it away."

I don't reprimand the nickname. There's actually something strangely sweet about it. I sit up straighter in the chair, clear my throat, and calm my head, preparing the story in my mind. With a deep breath, I begin reciting it from memory.

"'Christmas won't be Christmas without any presents,' grum- bled Jo, lying on the rug.'"

❧ 6 ❧

ANVIL

*W*hat if I fell head first in the shower? If I hit the tile just right, maybe that would end it all.

"Are you listening, Jay?" Melanie snaps.

I'm not. I never am when she's speaking. I hate her so much. I feel a fit of pique in my blood at how badly I wish she was the one suffering instead of me. I'll never respect or trust a social worker ever again after meeting her. Just like I'll never respect or trust a nurse after Nurse Ann. Never trust a hospital, never respect a doctor. It's too risky to think any health professional actually cares about your health.

This morning I looked at the offensive, chalky pills in the paper cup they gave me and knew I'd never look at orange medicine bottles with anything other than disdain again either. I'm not even sure how I'll manage to swallow antacids or antibiotics after this without cringing and gagging.

"I'm sorry," I mumble, ignoring Melanie's expression, forever incensed by my obvious sullenness. "What did you say?"

"I can't confidently say you should be released if it doesn't seem like you've made any progress."

"I have made progress."

"Your nurses and doctors report differently."

Of course they do. My dad's health insurance is the fancy kind. His company provides it. The hospital makes bank off of patients like me.

"Right," I say, staring at the hem of my paper clothes. "I'll try harder."

Maybe if I just fall face forward on the floor instead of the shower, it will have a better result. Melanie rattles on some more monotonous nonsense during our session. I spend the entire time plotting my own demise. Once we're finished, I head to the carpeted gym that smells like long forgotten basements and walk the track with Jenny, Stanley, Tracy, and the new kid on the block, Billy. He insists on wearing his laceless sneakers everywhere. They thump with every step, creating a recurrent rhythm to his walk. Jenny pretends he's beat boxing and makes up raps until a nursing intern yells at her to stop and focus on mindfulness during exercise hour. We walk our laps slower in protest until Billy succeeds in begging us to play basketball with him.

I'm surprisingly good at it.

We play HORSE.

I win by several letters.

The day drags on like every other day. My stalker's been released so at least I'm safe from that waking nightmare. The water still tastes like lead so my dehydration persists. The following morning Billy joins our trio in the medicine line, his shoes thumping along the linoleum.

"Give us a beat, Billy!" Jenny cheers.

Billy grins and begins to shuffle in place as Stanley and I shout: Go! Go! Go! while Jenny constructs another rap, this time the lyrics make jab after jab at this disgraceful excuse for a place of health and caring. Nurse Ann screams at us, announces to the entire room that she's making notes in our charts about our disorderly and disruptive behavior.

Billy's gone by the end of the day.
He's homeless.
He has no health insurance.

7

HAZARDOUS WEATHER

"Tell me something bad that happened while you were in the hospital."

I look up from my book of the day, *Emma*. Harriet has just arrived at Hatfield and I really don't feel like focussing on Laurie's absurd conversation starters when I could be consumed by the subtle sapphic brilliance of Jane Austen. I study his face, waiting for him to say 'nevermind' or laugh the question away, a joke on the winter wind. But the sun has fallen and the only thing keeping him illuminated is the glow from the fireplace. I have to squint to even make out the words on the page. I'm surely going to get a migraine if I keep at it. So I really have no choice but to indulge the Hatter on why a raven is like a writing desk.

I close the book, set it in my lap, keeping my eyes on Laurie. "Why?"

"Because I know bad things happened and I know most people don't care or don't believe you. But I care. I will believe you. And I will understand how those horrors felt. That's how we know each other. That's how you trust me."

"You sound so stupid," I huff. "This is the worst game of get-to-know-you ever."

I expect him to laugh but he remains earnest in this grisly pursuit.

"Jay, please."

"Fine." If he wants horror, I'll do my best to deliver. "This guy Tim had visual hallucinations and usually he saw bugs that weren't there. Mostly ants but sometimes spiders and beetles too. So he would check himself. He would ask me or my friend Jenny to confirm whether or not there was really a bug on the table or wherever he was, you know? But the problem was that the hospital had a bug problem. They were always getting in. Ants in the cafeteria, spiders in the beds, like something out of a nightmare simulation. And none of us could complain about it because then they'd just assume we were all hallucinating like Tim and then we risked the psychiatrist putting us on more intense meds. Well, one day Tim woke up and there were all these spiders in his bed and he screamed and the nurses came running and sedated him but not until after they dragged him into the hallway. We all saw it, it was horrifying. And we have no idea if there actually were spiders in his bed or not. But then I was terrified the same thing would happen to me and then everyone would have to watch me be dragged through the hall and sedated. And—" a sob gets trapped in my throat, I gasp. When did I get so emotional? "That's not care. That's not treatment. It's torture. And I guess it doesn't sound so awful when I explain it but—"

"It does."

Laurie's green eyes gaze into my blue ones but this time they don't burn. They radiate a warmth as soothing as the fireplace or the mug of peppermint tea. He shifts forward, wraps my hands up with his own. I don't pull mine away, I let him engulf my fingers in the gentle cradle of his own. The touch feels too comforting to be coming from hands that wielded a bloody ax less than twenty-four hours ago. They feel too familiar for someone I've never known before.

"It sounds horrifying, because it was. You have every right to feel horrified and traumatized and fucking furious about it. I care that it happened to you. I believe that it happened to you. And I hope every staff member in that hospital burns in hell. Do you see it now, Jay? *This* is how we know each other."

I shake my head. I don't want to accept his words. They're too fervent; radiating with a truth I can't accept. What would it say about Alice if she felt akin to the Hatter?

"What about you?" I ask. "Tell me something bad about what happened to you."

His expression falters, the fire flickering low, exposing fragments of his face to me. Like I'm speaking to a ghost.

"If I tell you," he says, "will it make us friends?"

I groan. "You're ridiculous. Fine, yes. We'll be best friends, forever connected by institutionalized trauma. Happy?"

He beams. "Exceedingly."

"All right then, bard." I lean back, pulling my hands free and waving one in his direction. "Take it away. Spin me a yarn."

Laurie looks sad to lose the touch of my skin against his, even if it was something as innocent as hand holding. I hate to admit that I miss the caress of his fingers too. But I refuse to be moved by this. Hand holding on a cold winter's night doesn't mean anything. Lots of people hold hands. It doesn't mean I think he's handsome or that I want to feel what it would be like to be held by him, wrapped up in those arms like loblolly branches.

"The first day there—" he begins, "—they made me line up with all the other patients for morning medicine. But I hadn't seen any doctor yet, I hadn't received a diagnosis, no evaluation had been done. When they gave me the pills I asked what they were, I was worried, you know? Taking mysterious meds. They said if I didn't take them there would be consequences. I asked to see a doctor, and they refused. I asked again what the pills were and why I had to take them. So they had two large male nurses tackle me to the ground while a female nurse sedated me. The giant needle jamming into my arm was more painful than I ever would've thought an injection could be. I woke up later strapped to a bed. I called for help. When no one came, I panicked. So I started screaming. That same fucking nurse came in and sedated me again. When I woke up the second time, she was standing over my bed, rattling the tiny paper cup with the pills inside. She asked if I was ready to behave."

Laurie's fingers twitch. Is he reaching out for me? I can't hold back anymore. His words are too dagger sharp. Ax heavy. I reach out and let him card his fingers through mine. He squeezes. I squeeze back.

"I nodded and she forced the pills down my throat without any water. Then she left me strapped to the bed for the rest of the day. I wet myself laying there, missed lunch and dinner. And then the pills made me sick, whatever they were. I threw up on myself. No one came to let me out or help me until morning. I spent the whole night laying in my own piss and vomit."

"Jesus fucking Christ, Laurie."

"Sometimes," he continues, "I wish that horror stories like this were few and far between. A rarity. But then I think about how many other people I was locked up with. How many hospitals there are in the world just like mine. And then there was you. When I looked at you and saw what you were wearing—those paper clothes, your shoes without laces—I knew immediately where you were from before I even saw the bracelet. And my heart broke. I knew something horrible must've happened to you. Something worse than what you've told me so far. And I was angrier than I've been in a long time."

"Angry for me?" No one's been angry on my behalf in a long time. Scared, hopeless, frustrated—yes. But enraged due to how I was being treated? No. Jenny and Stanley could hardly feel such a thing for me, they were too busy being angry for themselves. Commiserating is not the same as advocating.

Laurie nods. "Yes. All I could think when I carried you in here was how badly I wanted to protect you."

"From the hospital?"

"And the cops. And the world."

"And who's going to protect me from you?"

He squeezes my hands again. "You."

8
HAIL

Maybe I did fall off the roof.
I've been dead this whole time and this is hell.
Ghosts. Ghosts. Ghosts.

9

ATMOSPHERIC PRESSURE

When I wake the following morning, the snow is still ferociously bombarding the cabin and Laurie is gone. I find a still steaming mug of willow tea, a chocolate chip cookie, and a note on the kitchen table.

Went to gather herbs. Be back soon. -L.

I consume my bitter cup of tea, munching periodically on the cookie. I go to the bathroom to wash my face and reapply my bandages and then I retreat to the couch, returning to the pages of *Emma*. Several hours pass. I finish the book. I look through the box and select another title: *Peter Pan and Wendy.* A favorite, and Laurie's late friend's taste was excellent enough to select a copy of the tale with the original title, before the publishers demanded Wendy's name be dropped, dooming the story to only bear the moniker of the bloodthirsty brat who slaughtered so many lost boys grown old.

I finish the book before Laurie returns, snow-flushed with

a basket of foraged goods. He sets them on the table before turning to look at me with a smile like Wonderland.

"Come outside with me."

"Why?"

"Just trust me."

Doing so is very stupid. But I'm so bored and lonely and tired of words being my only company. I don Stanley's coat. Laurie uses some twine to make new laces for my boots and gives me his scarf so I can wrap it around my head to keep my ears warm. Together we head out into the snow. We walk down the steps, the icy slickness quelled by freshly spilt salt, the snowy down long since trodden by Laurie's boots.

"Ready?" he asks, still grinning.

"For what?"

Laurie grabs my hand and hurdles us backwards. I let out a very undignified squeak in response as we topple down into a soft mound of snow.

"Laurie, what the hell!"

"Snow angels! Come on, Birdy. Have some fun with me."

He releases my hand and begins to move his arms, flapping his snowy wings. I watch for a few seconds before a laugh bubbles up in my throat, escaping in a cloud of breathy arctic mist above us. I move my arms in tandem with his, creating an angel of my own. Snow continues to fall on us, dusting us in powdered sky sugar. It gets in my mouth and nose, coats my lashes, melts on my tongue.

We just keep laughing.

It feels so good to feel nothing but cold and happy. Eventually my body tires out. My arms stop moving halfway through their wing path, my eyes feeling droopy as a fatigue wave crashes to the shore of my body. Laurie rolls onto his side, his cheek pressed into the angel snow.

"Ready to go in?"

I nod. He jumps up first then helps me to stand. We walk

inside together, Laurie graciously supporting me as I hobble. Thankfully he doesn't make any demeaning offhand comment about my unstable spine and how easily it was taken down by a children's winter game.

"Let's have dinner," he says.

I sit at the table and watch as he melts snow for water, splitting it up between glasses for us to quench our thirst and a big pot to boil. He takes out a box of pasta, a jar of vodka sauce, and a bottle of red wine. He cooks with a precision I've never witnessed in any meal prep process. I imagine at fancy restaurants the chefs behave similarly behind their closed doors. Pay no attention to the man behind the curtain and all that. But here the Wizard is on full display with actual prowess.

Laurie sets the glass of snow water in front of me on the table along with another cookie. I consume both and then he gives me a cup of lavender tea. I sip it bit by bit, adding gobs of honey. I look to the box of books tucked away under the bed and decide to retrieve another. I return to the table with a copy of *Frankenstein* in my hands. One of my most read, most loved books. And by the looks of it Laurie's late friend loved it too; the pages and corners are more worn down and bent than any of the other paperbacks in the trove.

"Read to me." Laurie snaps the pasta in half in a manner that would appall many—I presume—and drops it in the pot.

I don't challenge him this time, just open the book and read

❧

AFTER DINNER AND A TALL GLASS OF WINE, I DOZE ON THE couch and

wake up late in the night to see Laurie standing at the window, staring at the falling snow. My eyes are heavy, weighed down by the red wine seeping through my system. I manage to pull myself off the couch and creep up to stand by his side. He remains silent. I watch the sugary flakes waft down from the stars, silently begging them to stop, to let me pass away from them to freedom.

Or a chance at freedom.

"Who's the superhero?" I ask.

Laurie turns his head slightly. "Hmm?"

"Yesterday, I saw a comic over there on the counter. I didn't recognize the person on the cover."

"Oh. Agent Peggy Carter. She's not a superhero, just a hero."

"No powers?"

He shakes his head. "No. She doesn't need them."

"Are you a big fan of hers?"

"Huge." He grins, rocking back on his heels, hands in his pockets. He looks like a kid who's just been granted candy for good behavior.

I haven't known many comic nerd men in my time but the few I have never boasted much of the female characters, let alone dedicated their reading material to solely them. I laugh, shake my head at the absurdity of it all. This place, this man, this racing in my chest and flush in my cheeks. I look at Laurie again, he's standing a bit closer, his features illuminated by the fire's glow, and damn it all.

"Give me your hand," he says softly.

I hold my hand out and let him hold it. He flips it over so my palm faces up then begins to trace the lines across my skin.

"Are you going to divine my future?"

He looks up at me from under those taunting brows, the Cheshire Cat consuming his smile once more. "Maybe, Birdy. Maybe. You see, my momma was a great diviner, sold her services and everything. She taught me how to read tea leaves poorly and palms very well. But I'm sure someone like you, all logic and sense, doesn't believe in something as woo woo as fortune telling."

His tone needles me, the words pinpricks on my skin. What a childish challenge, and still I feel the need to face it.

I harden my jaw, tilting my head back to easily hold his stare. "I believe in compelling evidence."

"All right then, darling." He drags a finger down the center of my hand. My skin reacts too strongly to his feathery touch. I feel a jolt in my stomach. Butterflies riot against the walls of my ribcage. Skipped the caterpillar hookah stage all together.

"You're going to live a long life. Oh, the irony."

He chuckles. I slam my shoulder against his. Playfully. A hop, skip, and a jump away from flirting. The firelight and starlight seem to shine brighter, forcing me to face the truth of the moment, own up to my own active participation in whatever this is. Whatever we're becoming.

"You'll live to be a hundred and two." He taps my palm in confirmation.

"I'm holding you to that. If I die even a day before my 102nd birthday, my ghost will come haunt you."

"You really think little old me is still going to be kicking at a hundred?"

I bite my lip, a smile escaping between my clenched teeth. "You better be. I'm not going to keep facing this nonsense world

alone."

I can't explain myself, I'm afraid, Sir. Because I am not myself, you see.

Laurie keeps tracing lines on my palms, speaking softly. His words lose all sense. I'm lost in those stupidly green eyes.

"You're staring." He smirks.

"You're hard to look away from." I speak without thinking. His smirk turns into a wild grin and I know there's no taking it back.

He holds my hand between both of his, a stack of palms and unspoken predictions.

"You're impossible to look away from." "Laurie."

"Yes?"

Curiouser and curiouser.

"I think you should kiss me."

"I do too."

Laurie shifts, leaning down closer, his arboraceous scent; a mix of pine needles and merlot. His lips find mine, both of ours a bit chapped and cracked from the cold, but still soft and warm, tongues still stained by the wine, yet overall our mouths fit together perfectly. Flawlessly. He presses his tongue to the seam of my lips, I part them—eagerly. My mouth welcomes his tongue on its plundering mission. His hands tangle in my messy hair, my chest expands with my stuttered breath, our bodies meld together, melted into one by the fire. I grab onto his arms, holding on for balance, for stability, for madness. His kiss turns feverish and feral. I happily drown in the sensation.

We continue on and on until one of my knees triggers, a spasm rocketing across the surface. I gasp from the onslaught of pain, my legs buckling out from under me, but Laurie's hands are there to catch me. He wraps me up in his arms and carries me to the couch where he lays me down with the same reverence I used to see the nuns treat religious idols in church growing up. The couch is the altar and I'm a figure of the Virgin Mary laid out on its surface before the Holy Sacrament. Laurie completes the picture by kneeling down in front of me, hands resting on my knees.

"Are you okay?" he asks softly.

"Yeah. My knee spasmed for a second, but I'm fine now." Laurie's fingers find their way back into my hair, twirling the wavy strands around his skin. Autumn leaves dancing in the firelight.

"If you're ever in too much pain to keep on doing something just tell me, okay? I'm not going to judge you or be a jerk about it or anything."

"I'm not in too much pain to kiss you."

He smiles, tugs lightly on my hair. "That's excellent news." Laurie shifts forward and captures my mouth with his, nipping at my bottom lip until a breathy whimper escapes from the back of my throat.

"That was a pretty sound." He grazes his nose along mine, fingers tracing circles along the column of my throat. "Can you make it again?"

"I don't know." I smile against his mouth. "Try."

Laurie's eyes glimmer, his lashes close enough to butterfly kiss mine. He tangles his hands deep in my hair and pushes me back onto the couch until I'm laying flat and his body's on top of me. He makes sure to keep his weight balanced so as not to crush me. He releases my hair to caress my jaw with one hand, the other used to maintain his balance above me.

"Tell me to stop," he whispers, his words nothing but dragon breath.

I reach up and tangle my own hands in his hair, pulling a bit less than lightly on his dark locks. He groans softly, eyes closing in a strange expression of peace. Of trust.

"No." My voice is just loud enough to be heard over the crackling of the fire. "I don't want you to."

Laurie opens his eyes again, stares at me from his propped position. "Birdy—" he cups my jaw, using his thumb to push my head back, keeping me in place, keeping my eyes locked on him. "—are you still afraid of me?"

You're nothing but a pack of cards.

A soft smile creeps like a caterpillar across my lips. I shake my head, hair splayed out around my head in a fiery halo. "No, Laurie. I'm not."

"Thank God. I've been going mad waiting."

He descends on me before I can demand he clarify what he was waiting for.

The answer is clear.

Me.

Oh how far Alice has fallen.

I shift my legs to accommodate Laurie's body between my hips, his want strained against his jeans. My own desire courses through me resulting in my hips tilting up to meet him with beautiful friction. We shift together like that for a small eternity. Kisses and sighs, fully clothed grinding bodies, sweaty palms caressing sweaty cheeks. There's something wonderfully immature about the whole thing. Like two teenagers falling in love on a muggy summer night, no idea that the entire world is lurking just around the corner, waiting to end them.

We eventually begin to remove our clothes. We whisper requests for permission to do away with sweaters, then jeans, then underwear, laughing at the idea of truly being stripped down to our socks.

"Good God, look at you," Laurie breathes, sitting back on his heels to drink in the sight of me, splayed out like a feast before him.

My body tingles, what was once a slowly blooming yearning for him has overgrown and consumed me over the course of a few hours drunk off his touches. I feel aglow beneath his gaze. It's been so long since any man looked at me like a sexually desirable being. If they did dare to consider me in such a way, the second they caught sight of my cane all notions of pursuing me vanished. No one courts the disabled girl, this I have sorely learned. Now I can't seem to remember how those rejections felt. Not under Laurie's green-eyed gaze.

"I'm...I'm not on birth control," I say almost shamefully. "And I'm assuming you didn't bring condoms out here for your whole lumberjack, cottagecore experience."

He chuckles. I've grown to love that laugh these past few days. It's fallen on me as heavy as blizzard blown snow.

"We don't need to worry about all that then." He shifts forward again, lips hovering over mine, one hand snaking down the center of my body until it rests above my core, dangerously close to where I so badly want to feel him. "Can I touch you?"

I nod, wrapping my arms around his neck, bringing his lips crashing back down to mine. Waves upon my shore. Laurie's fingers start by lightly dancing through the red patch of hair between my thighs, tugging gently here and there, driving me mad with arousal until I'm a pathetic, writhing mess of want beneath him.

"Laurieeee." I whine dramatically, achieving another throaty laugh from his lovely, loblolly lips.

His fingers slide inside and that's the end of me. I become a supernova of light. My body floats above this lousy world, I walk on the air, I dance with the snow. Any pain I once felt in my bones is long forgotten, for this is the most beautiful form of dissociation I've ever felt. I push my hips up further and further, wanting his hand to become one with my pelvic floor. I want my opening to swallow up his fingers and knuckles and bones and his blood to blend with mine. All my logic has burned away, turned to ash in the fire.

Down, down, down Alice fell.

Such a long way down.

But it's so pretty here where, for the first time in eight months, someone is touching me with something other than hate.

I feel a surge of unprecedented emotion overwhelm me as my peak builds higher and higher between my legs from the dance Laurie's fingers have choreographed between my shaking thighs. I finish with a soft cry, burying my head into the crook of his neck.

"I'm sorry," I whisper. "I can't believe I'm crying. I enjoyed it, really, I don't know why I feel—"

"Hey." Laurie takes my chin in between his spindle fingers, the warm and worn pads of his thumb and forefinger keeping me in place. "It's okay. I've been there too."

"Have you read *Alice's Adventures in Wonderland?*" Is my brilliantly poetic response.

He smiles, a soft laugh traveling from his mouth to my mind. "When I was a kid. We're all mad here, yes, I know, Birdy."

I Cheshire-smile myself for once. I reach up and push some of his floppy curls out of his eyes. "All right, Hatter."

He winks, kisses my forehead.

Time has frozen, but unlike the tea party residents in the story, I think I'm quite content to stay here for just a little while longer.

Until the snow clears.

❧ 10 ❧

ANABATIC WIND

"*Glory to God in the highest!*" *Jenny cheers as she walks into the room for Reflection Hour. She's waving a pack of colored pencils in the air. "Got the goods!"*

"And you thought that was worthy of praising God?" I ask.

She sits down across from me at the small table. "You said you were Catholic."

I roll my eyes. "I said I was raised Catholic."

Jenny shrugs. "Same difference."

She opens the paper box and spills the pencils across the table. A meager rainbow. Compared to the tedious and impossible-feeling sudoku sheet in front of me this is a world of possibilities. Jenny flips over my paper and the one I laid out for her so that the blank side is facing up. She pushes some of the pencils my way, a smile dancing across her mouth. It's such a beautiful sight, one rarely seen by anyone in here. I'm a terrible drawer so I stick to mostly doodling flowers, suns, and spirals, but it's peaceful to do something with the sole intent of creating beauty for the first time in ages. I peer across the table to get a look at Jenny's.

"Oh wow," I breathe. "Jenny, that's gorgeous."

She looks up at me, proud, beaming. "Yeah?"

I nod fervently. Jenny's drawn a stunning butterfly with great, big, swooping wings shaded in yellow and green. It takes up the entire sheet of paper, demanding attention, banishing the sudoku numbers on the other side to obscurity. It's the loveliest thing.

"I love that, Jenny. Can I...can I keep it?"

She grins wider. "Sure! You really like it that much?" "Absolutely. Make sure you sign it."

Jenny keeps grinning as she scribbles an artist's signature on the corner of the page then delightedly presents it to me. I don't want to risk it getting confiscated or thrown away so I fold the small sheet of paper up as tiny as I can and slip it inside my pocket.

"Remember me when you're a famous artist," I say. Jenny laughs.

ICY ROADS

I wake sometime later, drenched in lavender morning sunlight, wrapped up in a quilt and Laurie's arms. I sigh, feeling remarkably safe for how dangerous he is and how precarious the state of my life has become.

Then I realize.

The snow has stopped falling.

The storm's ended.

"Laurie." I excitedly nudge him awake. "Laurie, wake up! It's stopped snowing!"

Laurie opens groggy eyes. "Hey there, Birdy."

He kisses my temple.

"It's stopped snowing," I repeat. "We can go into town. I can call my sister."

His glowing eyes dim slightly. Now is the moment of truth.

To see if he really is a terrifying beast I should fear, ready to keep me trapped here, or just a friendly hobbit who slays dragons in the form of corrupt cops.

"Let's get dressed. There's a diner in town where we can get breakfast."

Dragon-slaying hobbit it is.

We bundle up as best we can. I triple check that Jenny's drawing is still in the pocket of Stanley's coat, Laurie gives me some willow bark to chew on, and we head out. His truck is parked behind the cabin. It's a small vehicle, certainly not made to withstand harsh, snowy conditions, and I wonder how it's even going to get us to the road.

"Don't worry." He opens the passenger side door for me. "The tires have decent tread. There's some back paths hikers and campers use around here, they'll lead us to the main road and then it's a smooth drive into town."

Laurie helps me clamber into the truck and we're off. We don't have to drive for very long over bumpy, snowy paths before we reach the edge of the treeline with glorious asphalt laying beyond it.

Except...

"No," I whisper.

"Fuck," Laurie breathes. "Wait here."

He parks the truck, gets out, and walks to the edge of the road.

I watch through misty eyes as he crouches down to place a hand on the road, testing it. But I can see even from here it's covered in a layer of thick ice, far too much for any civilian vehicle to safely drive across. It would only take one wrong move for us to go skidding off the road and I doubt the Fates will let me be lucky enough to survive two car crashes in less than a week's time.

I get out and join Laurie by his side. He looks up at me from his crouch, his eyes weary. "I'm so sorry, Jay."

"Can we walk?" I ask. "How far is it to town?" He stands up straight. "Three miles."

My heart stops beating.

Three miles.

Without a cane. Without any proper pain medicine. On

the uneven snowy forest floor, weighed down by Stanley's bulky coat. My eyes get misty again. But I have to try, don't I? I have to get back to Katrina—have to get back to freedom.

"I'll help you." Laurie takes my hand. "I'll keep you steady."

I sniff back more tears, smile through my fear. "Okay, Hatter. Let's give this Caucus Race a go."

He forces a laugh. We head off into the frosty unknown.

We don't even make it a mile before my entire body feels aflame and I'm practically leaning all my weight against Laurie's side. He's doing his best to keep me steady, holding me upright as straight as he can. But it's no use, my body hates me for this endeavor. Soon enough a burning spasm shoots from the base of my skull all the way to my feet and I go down. Laurie catches me, but he's exhausted too. Together we topple into the snow.

I sob.

I can't help it anymore. Everything is just too much. Too painful. Too hard. Too cold. Too endless.

"Hey." Laurie takes my face in his hands. "Jay, I *will* get you home, alright? It just looks like we can't make that happen today. But in a day or two they'll plow the roads and then we can drive into town easily and gorge ourselves on waffles at the diner. You'll be able to call your sister, she'll come get you, and everything will be alright."

I shake my head, tears falling and freezing. "No, it's—"

"*Yes*, Jay. I'm promising you now that I will get you there. Okay?"

He's so adamant. So sure. So determined.

Determined to help *me*, of all people.

I nod. "Okay."

He nods too, bringing my face closer and kisses my forehead, his lips warm against my chilled body. A lavender sun against my snow-soaked skin.

WE DRIVE BACK TO THE CABIN WITHOUT SPEAKING AND remain silent as we re-enter. Laurie gets to work making scrambled eggs and tea for us. I sit at the table and watch him, not even able to bring myself to read as a distraction. My mind is horribly present. Once Laurie puts a big plate of eggs and a huge mug of black tea in front of me and settles across from me, I finally shatter our stalemate of silence.

"Will you tell me why you got sent away?"

Laurie takes a bite of eggs. Keeps his stare unblinking as he chews. I sip my scalding tea. Laurie swallows loud enough to cause an avalanche.

"Come on," I insist. "I've told you everything about me."

"That's not true. You've only told me bits and pieces. Only shared scraps of yourself with me. I know you love literature and your sister. That you're eternally grumpy and don't believe in destiny or fate. And I know how good your body feels against mine, but do I really know you, Jay Dove?"

"You know I'm crazy like you."

The corner of his mouth lifts up in an almost smile.

"You're not crazy like me, Jay. I'm far worse than you, you know that."

"If I know that, then you have nothing to lose by telling me." He finishes the rest of his eggs, gulps down half his mug of tea, lays his palms flat on the table, his fingers sliding so close to mine. An ocean separates one side of the table from the other. I don't know if I'm a strong enough swimmer to cross it.

"My sister, Florence. I killed her boyfriend."

"Why?"

"Why do you think? Because he hurt her. She kept trying to leave him and it never worked. She would hide away at friends' apartments and extended family members' houses but he always found her. She went to the police and got a restraining order, he ignored it and the cops didn't care when she reported it. And then he would show up with flowers and a pitiful apology and she took him back every time. Maybe it was just fear of him doing worse to her if he had to hunt her down again, maybe she actually loved him—I don't know. But I knew I couldn't stomach coming home to see my sister painted in any more bruises."

"Why a mental hospital though?" I ask. "And not just regular prison."

Laurie's fingers inch a bit further across the table.

"I thought Florence told me to kill her boyfriend. I thought she was standing in the room with me telling me to do it. I thought she handed me the knife. I thought she was so happy, watching me kill that evil man. But when it was done I realized I was alone in the kitchen and I was covered in his blood. I heard the front door open. I was so confused, we lived alone. I looked in the doorway and my sister wasn't there anymore. I panicked. But you know what happened, don't you?"

"She was never really there," I whisper.

His fingers twitch, nervously tapping the table. I suspect it has been a very long time since he's told this story.

'Call the first witness,' said the King; and the White Rabbit blew three blasts on the trumpet, and called out, 'First witness!'

His forehead is slick with sweat even though the fire is burning very low in the hearth and the sun has settled lower in the sky. His twitching fingers wrap around his mug of tea, sip more of the now surely lukewarm liquid.

The first witness was the Hatter. He came in with a teacup in one hand and a piece of bread–and–butter in the other. 'I beg pardon, your Majesty,' he began, 'for bringing these in: but I hadn't quite finished my tea when I was sent for.'

I don't want to be his Queen of Hearts questioning him until he loses his mind.

A mind already lost.

I don't want to ruin him any more than this world has already ruined him. Same way it's ruined me.

We're late for a very important date, Laurie Hatter.

I slide my arm across the table and take his hand in mine, lacing our fingers up until they settle together, knuckles to knuckles, skin to skin, making some logic and sense out of the madness simmering at this poor excuse for a tea party.

"It's okay," I say gently. "Keep going."

His brow unfurrows a bit, he takes a shaky breath, nods.

"It was her I heard at the door, she was coming home from work. She found me in the kitchen and screamed. It was an awful sound. She kept saying, '*what did you do?*' And I kept trying to explain that I had saved her, that this was what she wanted. She ran out of the room, I heard her throwing up. I knew she wouldn't call the cops on me, she would help me get rid of the body. I didn't want to put that burden on her. So I got the electric knife we used to carve turkey on Thanksgiving."

My hand squeezes Laurie's too hard.

This confession has turned grisly. This fairytale turned horror story.

"I started cutting him up." He continues without faltering. "I know my sister heard me. She came in and started screaming at me that I had to stop. The neighbors must have heard the screaming because they called the police. When we heard the sirens she was so panicked, talking so fast, saying we had to come up with a story. But what could we say? There was no way to hide what I'd done, and I was so deluded, my brain refusing to agree on what it was actually seeing and hearing. She tried to wrestle the electric knife from me, but I was worried if she got it then she would get partially blamed for what I'd done. I fought her. And...I cut her. Accidentally. But it was bad. By the time the cops came in and hauled me away, I couldn't make sense of what I was seeing, or fully remember what I had done. I was covered in blood. All over. When I went to trial they pulled up my past history of mental illness, delusions and hallucinations. When they recounted the crime scene and the state I was found in, it didn't match what I thought had happened. Not completely. It was a quick trial, an easy decision."

"What didn't match?" I whisper.

"I had blood on my mouth, Jay."

I remain silent in his arms and let the words settle around me. My mouth falls open in a silent gasp when the pieces of his puzzle finally snap into place. I try to let go of his hand but he holds onto me tightly.

"Laurie, what the fuck? That's so—"

"Sick? Yes, I know. I *am* sick. But you know places like that don't make people like me any better."

"I know that but—"

"I didn't do it on purpose. It's not like I actively decided to try and eat his dead body. Apparently I never cut my sister. She never wrestled the knife from me. She was pulling me off his body."

"I don't understand."

"Me either. No one is more baffled by my mind than me. Maybe I thought it was the only way to get rid of the body and protect her."

"What? Like you're a fucking zombie?"

There's silence. It hurts. It terrifies me. And then we both begin to laugh, twitching teacup fingers gripping each other fiercely. It's too absurd. Our stories, our trauma, our truth. How can two people like us have possibly found their way to each other?

"It wasn't the first time I tried to kill myself," I say, the words falling like a tower of cards from my lips. "I tried once before. Took a bunch of pills. Cliche, I know. I was only seventeen. My sister, Katrina, found me on the bathroom floor and got me to throw them up before it was too late."

"Sisters are strong creatures, aren't they?"

"Very much so."

"Why did you want to die then?"

I grip his hand a little bit harder. A tether to a semblance of stability. "I was being bullied. It was high school. It's not an original reason."

"That doesn't make it any less valid. Why did you try to jump this time?"

"The pain. I was going mad from it. And then one day it just swooped down on me like a hungry vulture. This ever present reminder that I would have this pain in my body forever, that there's no real cure for DDD or fibromyalgia and that no medical professional would ever really try to help me. I got on the roof of our apartment building, got on the ledge, and was about to jump when I heard my mom screaming behind me. I blacked out and woke up strapped to a gurney in an ambulance."

Laurie is silent, his eyes searching mine for some kind of epiphany.

"You're not going to leave this place with the passing of the storm, are you?" I ask.

"No." He shakes his head. "Not for a while at least."

"How do you even have money for all your food and supplies? How will you continue to get money?"

"The friend whose cabin this was had an emergency stash of cash. After that runs out, I'll make a call and get set up with a job that doesn't ask too many questions. Pays in cash. Stay out here where no one will think to look. Make sure to stock up in the winter."

Make a call. Someone on the inside must have connections

they shared with him before his escape. The kind of connections I've only ever seen in movies. Ambiguous and unset-
tling. I can't press him for more information, it will only send
me off kilter and I'm so close to feeling balanced for the first
time in ages. He's able to keep me on this tightrope with such
ease, it makes no sense. Pure madness. But who am I to
demand logic and reason?

I release his hand, get up, and go settle myself on his lap.
He doesn't hesitate in wrapping his arms around my waist. I
gently trace the curve of his razor-sharp jaw, count the gold
flecks in his green eyes. A beautiful, glowing, ambery copse of
color.

I embrace the madness and whisper: "I'm glad I met you."

Laurie twists a lock of my hair around his finger; fire in his
hands.

Unstoppable force of a man.

"Me too."

We kiss. Logic melts away. I let insanity consume me.

❦

"WHAT DO YOU DO ALL DAY?" I ASK.

Laurie looks up from where he sits at the kitchen table
sorting through his recently foraged herbs. I'm lounging on
the couch, flicking through the pages of *Dracula*. I don't like
this book but beggars can't be choosers and I need a story to
latch onto.

Laurie shrugs. "Walk, keep the cabin stocked with firewood and herbs, read that Agent Carter comic. I plan to get
more comics in town when we're able to get there. Sleep. I
sleep a lot."

"Why don't you read any of the books?"

He clenches his jaw. His fingers grip the leaves he's
holding too hard and they crumble in his hands.

"Not a big reader." He returns his attention to the leaves.

A few hours and bowls of freshly cooked pasta later we decide it's time for bed. Laurie settles in on the couch, me in the actual bed. The fire simmers down low, the night settles around us. I lay in the darkness, staring at the ceiling, feeling so entirely lonely.

"Laurie?"

"Jay." Of course he's still awake.

I sit up in bed to find that he's already sitting up on the couch, looking at me. I don't say anything, just push back the covers on the far side of the bed, my eyes boring into his with desperate earnestness. He remains silent himself as he gets up and crawls into bed beside me. He lays on his side, I settle into his arms with perfect sense. Our bodies fit together the way the last piece of a jigsaw puzzle snaps into place. There's a feeling of perfect harmony between us.

"What happened?" he says, his voice softly traveling through the darkness.

"What do you mean?"

"Why did you decide to escape?"

The silence I create suffocates me. Laurie doesn't push me to rush an answer, or to even answer at all. My mind reels, clocks ticking so loud I could go deaf. The memories crawl their way out of the corners of my mind. All the moments behind those walls I promised myself I would never give power to by speaking. All the hateful words said by the staff, the horrific sights of friends being tackled and sedated in the hall as they screamed and begged, and *him*. How he found me in the hallway. And then when he checked back in. When freedom became nothing but a memory.

"Some things you just can't speak about," I whisper.

He tightens his hold on me, pulling me in closer to his sweet, pine scent. He doesn't say anything else. He just understands. *Finally* someone understands.

Laurie's gone when I wake, leaving a note about going to chop more firewood. He left me some toast and tea. I nibble and sip my breakfast, pull out the old box and hunt for another book. I'm running low on options. I open a copy of *Jane Eyre* and a picture flutters from the pages into my lap. I set the book down, pick up the picture. My heart stops. It's a picture of a younger Laurie, grinning, arms wrapped around a girl who looks so much like him, she must be Florence. There's a woman standing behind them with very similar features. She's smiling, hands on each of their shoulders. They're outside in the photo, it's clearly spring or summer, and they're standing in front of the cabin. The hobbit hole. The only safe place for miles and miles in these viscous woods.

His friend.

Laurie's friend who killed themself and left him this cabin if he ever needed it.

The stash of money.

The supply of food.

His mother.

"Jay?"

I look up, tears in my eyes. Laurie's standing in the doorway

with those beautifully frost-flushed cheeks and an armful of firewood.

"Are you all right?" His eyes travel from my face to my hands where the picture is nestled between my shaking fingers. "Oh." His voice is so soft and hollow.

"I'm so sorry," I whisper.

Laurie puts the firewood down and slowly strides over to stand before me. He crouches down, coming onto his knees. I offer him the picture, a holy sacrament between us. He takes it tenderly, thumbing the bent corner, eyes glazing over as he gazes at the memory captured by light.

"Where did you find this?" he asks. I point to the copy of *Jane Eyre*. He smiles. "That was her favorite. She read the entire thing to me once. Gloomy stuff."

"Yes," I say. "But romantic."

Laurie looks up from the photo. "Like us." "Yes, Laurie. Like us."

❧ 12 ❧

FREEZING

J enny and Stanley are both sporting horrified expressions as they sit down across from me at breakfast. I look up from the soggy excuse for a pancake I've been poking with my fork for ten minutes. I'm so hungry my stomach aches but the food here is barely edible. Eating too much of it almost always results in vomiting and that's a dangerous thing here. You don't want to get Eating Disorder added to your file or they'll have another reason to abuse you, extend your stay, make your life a worse living hell than it already is.

Dante's got nothing on this place.

"What is it?" I ask.

"He's back," Jenny says. "Checked back in this morning."

I drop my plastic fork. "What?"

"Apparently as soon as he got home he tried to walk into traffic and when his roommate went out to stop him he tried to drag them into traffic with him."

My stomach is full of rocks. I'm the Wolf in Red Riding Hood's tale and I'm surely bound to drown soon. Jenny and Stanley's words weigh me down, deeper and deeper I sink with no hope of ever seeing the surface again.

I miss the sun.

☙❧

Jenny sits beside me during nightly Reflection Time, only an hour until mandatory lights out, though the lights never go out for me, Tracy, and all the others sentenced to sleep on cots in the hall. A place where he can find me just like last time. Corner me out of the nurse's sight. Even if I told my dad again and he stormed in here and raged at them again to protect me, they never will. No one cares about crazy girls, this I have finally learned.

"Did you ever notice," Jenny says, "that Nurse Ann leaves her keys right by her computer, like, all the time?"

I turn slowly to face Jenny. She has her eyes glued to the stereo across the room where the abrasive waterfall sounds are playing.

"Yeah?" I keep my voice low, turning my own gaze to the stereo, making sure to move my lips as little as possible.

Jenny gives a curt nod. "Yeah."

Stanley enters the room, roughly pushed in by several orderlies. He almost crashes to his knees with their force, but he's a big guy and able to regain his balance. He scans the room, spies the empty seat on the other side of me. He makes a beeline for it. Settles in. I watch as he and Jenny share a look across me.

"I keep forgetting to hang up my coat," Stanley says. "I always mean to wear it to Exercise Hour, sweat off some of this weight, but I just leave it laying on my bed."

"That's funny," Jenny says.

"Yeah." I nod. "Never noticed it before."

"You know that new orderly? Kyle, I think his name is." Stanley finally looks directly at me. I nod. "Well, he gets off at eight every night. Works a second job, he told me so the other day after he— well..."

When he and several other orderlies tackled Stanley to the floor and sedated him for being 'violent' and 'disorderly.'

He was having a panic attack. PTSD. From what, we'll never know. I'm sure he's told the doctors, even more sure that they don't care. And the mysterious, chalky, white pills we all down every morning clearly do nothing to help. There is no help here. Just nine circles of hell. Dante, Dante, can you hear us?

"I think he goes out the back hall," Jenny says, her voice turning to a whisper. "The one by the medicine counter."

Stanley bumps my shoulder in a familiar, playful nature but this time it's clearly a performance. He smiles and fake laughs, slipping something into my hand as he does. I peer down, unfurl my fingers the tiniest bit. It's a small piece of wood. A doorstop. I feel tears prick my lashes but I blink them away quickly. Being seen crying is the worst of all. There's no getting out for crazies who cry.

"It's been wonderful knowing you, Jay." I look into Jenny's eyes, they're beaming and bright. She means it.

I nod, sniffling. "You too, Jenny."

But I don't want to stop knowing her. We have to find our way back to each other. All three of us. I'd hug her and Stanley if I could, but touching is strictly forbidden. If we were seen embracing, we'd end up in solitary confinement, heavily sedated for sure.

"It's probably cold outside," Stanley adds. "Hope folks heading out are bundled up."

I check the clock. Fifteen minutes until Kyle gets off work. I excuse myself to go to the bathroom, looking back over my shoulder at my friends. They don't dare wave to me, but their eyes say it all. Unspoken goodbyes hanging from our lips. They're saving me in a way I'll never be able to save them. I head past the bathroom to where Stanley's room is. He's left the door open. I slip in and grab his coat off the bed, pulling it on. I remove my one belonging from my paper pocket and tuck it away safely in the coat's warm one instead.

The paper butterfly flaps its wings in encouragement.

I can do this.

I head back out to the main room, praying no one notices the coat I'm wearing. I make my way to the counter, Nurse Ann is on break so I ask Nurse Debra for some sudoku sheets. She grumbles but goes to get me some. As soon as her back's turned I reach forward and snatch Nurse Ann's keys, tucking them in my pocket along with the butterfly, the door jamb still hidden in my clenched fist.

Nurse Debra comes back with the sudoku sheets, I accept them with a fake smile, taking a tiny pencil from the cup. As I'm walking back to Jenny and Stanley, I hastily scribble my number on the back of one of the sheets. I pass them out to my friends, ignoring their worried stares. The clock ticks away, 7:55. I need to go. But Nurse Ann is back from break, watching us with a hawklike stare. I'll never be allowed to slip past the medicine counter.

"Stanley," Jenny whispers.

"Remember me fondly, dollface." Stanley smiles at me, then gets up, walks to the center of the room and pretends to have one of his episodes.

The nurses start screaming, calling for orderlies. Other patients join in the madness. Jenny squeezes my hand and I run. I round the corner to the back hall just as Kyle is slipping away, clearly wanting to leave without having to be dragged into the chaos currently unfolding on my behalf. I run after him as quietly as I can manage with my clunking boots. I slide the wooden jamb across the floor, it makes its way in between the closing door and the latch just in time, just enough. I open the door, kick the jamb aside and let the winter air chill my face, freeze my bones. I hear more screaming coming from the main room. I glance back over my shoulder at the sound, but I can't go back, I can't help them. Right now I have to help myself.

I step outside and run.

Laurie isn't in the bed when I wake. I sit up and see him on the couch with something that looks like a wooden cane in his hands.

"Laurie."

He looks up, smiles. I realize what he's holding in his other hand, a knife. He's been whittling the wood, carving and shaping it. I get out of bed and start to walk over to him.

"Did you make that?" I ask softly.

"I know it's not as good as a real cane, but I figured—" Before he can get another word out I collapse into him, wrapping my arms around his neck, burying my face in his shoulder. He wraps his arms around my back, pressing his fingers against the fabric of my shirt, nuzzling his nose into my hair.

"It's wonderful," I whisper. "So, so wonderful."

"You know what else is?"

I pull away from the safe space of his neck and sweet smelling hair to look into his gorgeous green eyes. "What?"

"I went to check the road while you were sleeping. The ice has melted."

AN HOUR LATER WE'RE DRIVING DOWN THE CLEARED ROAD, zooming away from the hobbit hole and towards town, a trove of unknowns before us. I almost cried when we left. I know I can't hide out in the hobbit hole and become a hermit forever. But how marvelous might it be to consider? A world of our own where nonsense reigns and the weight of the real world melts away, dissolves like sugar lumps in teacups. We could become legends, the great crazy beasts lurking in the woods. Teenagers would tell scary stories about us at sleepovers and bonfires, daring each other to come knock on our door.

But I'm not like Laurie. I may have committed crimes but not anything like what he's done. If I can get to Katrina, then there can be hope for me yet. And maybe Jenny and Stanley will get out soon and we can find our way to each other again just like I've always hoped. But the question is will I be able to ever find my way to Laurie again? I want to ask him but I know he won't give me an honest answer, if he'll give me any at all. So I settle into the silence. He drives with one hand on the wheel and the other on my knee, keeping me steady as the car trundles over the rocky roads. We arrive in the one horse town and pull into a diner parking lot. I use my new cane, grateful to finally take some strain off my joints. Once inside, Laurie orders us coffee and pancakes. The waitress smiles as she brings our meal. After we've had our fill, Laurie slides his burner phone across the table to me and I excuse myself to go to the bathroom and call Katrina. The phone rings twice before she answers.

"Hello?"

"Katrina? It's Jay."

"Oh my God! Jay! What the hell? Oh my God, I've been so

worried. Mom and Dad called and said you went missing, and Jay, Jesus Christ, did you steal a car? They said there was a crash and that they couldn't find you and then the cops went missing in the storm and—"

"I didn't see any cops," I lie. "I found this empty cabin in the woods near a town. That's where I've been. I waited until the storm passed and the roads were less icy." Katrina makes a huffing sound that says she knows I'm leaving a lot out of my story. "I'm okay-ish. I hurt my head in the crash. I hit some ice."

"Why did you run away? I could've done something."

I sigh and rest my head against the dirty bathroom wall. "Like what? They kept finding reasons to extend my stay to make money off Dad's insurance. They kept lying to Mom and Dad, saying my behavior was getting worse. Katrina, I need your help. I can't go back. I know the car theft charge is bad, but I'm telling you now, if I end up having to walk back in there, it will be the same as walking into my grave."

There's a long pause and I panic, thinking maybe the line has gone dead.

Then I hear Katrina take a shaky breath. "I'll help you. Where are you? I'm coming to get you."

Five minutes later I return to the table and my legs give out at the sight. The waitress rushes over to help me stand and there's murmurs of concern as she helps me into my seat and asks me if I need anything. I tell her I'm fine, tell her my ride will be here soon, even though it's going to take Katrina several hours. I sit at the empty table and stare at the two coffee cups. One in front of me and one in front of the empty seat where Laurie was. He ate all his pancakes before he disappeared. The only thing that he left behind is enough money to cover my bill and then some, and a napkin with some pen scribbled on it. I pick it up, my hand shaking.

Birdy, fly away. Be free.

By the time Katrina shows up at the diner, the sun has set and I've cried myself sick. I crash into her arms, my heart breaking for more reasons than I can say.

❧ 14 ❧

WEATHER PATTERNS

ONE YEAR LATER

I got a year of community service. Katrina is an excellent lawyer. Not excellent enough though to help me succeed in getting the hospital shut down. I spend my nights researching countless stories online from survivors of mental hospital malpractice and abuse. They're endless. They're agonizing. They're all too familiar.

Jenny never calls.

I still wear Stanley's coat when it's cold.

I taped Jenny's butterfly drawing up above my bed. I press my fingers to it before I go to sleep. Then I touch the old napkin I keep tucked away in my pillowcase.

My parents walk around me like I'm made of glass, the floor at my feet nothing but eggshells. I told Katrina some of what happened, that a hiker found me, helped me. She keeps my secret from our parents. They're racked with guilt, they say so at every mandatory therapy session the court ordered we attend as a family unit. I call Katrina often. My head hurts. My heart hurts. I check the paper for obituaries. I check my mind to make sure I didn't make it all up.

The answers always come back inconclusive.

❧

I MOVE OUT OF MY PARENTS' HOUSE JUST IN TIME FOR winter to rear its ugly head. I get a job at the comic shop in the one horse town. I tell them I need space, need escape. They don't understand. I start a blog about being a mental hospital survivor and post constantly about Jenny and Stanley. I never hear from them. Maybe they're still in there. Maybe they're in the ground. Laurie's words play on a loop in my mind.

People like us die all the time.

When the first snow of the season starts to fall like fresh sugar I see a familiar, loblolly figure leaving the diner next door as I'm getting off my shift. He's walking to that familiar truck with its weak wheels, unable to traverse ice. I knew there was no chance I'd be able to find my way to the cabin again on my own, and my car certainly can't handle those woodsy roads. But I knew he must have to come into town sometimes. And here he is. *Finally.* I don't call out his name, he might be using a different one in town. Might have faked his own death.

Might have, might have, might have.

I shuffle quickly across the frosty ground, my cane clicking against the asphalt of the joint parking lot. "Hatter!"

He freezes, his back to me. I hurry over until I'm only a few feet away. "Birdy?" he whispers.

"It's me."

He turns around, his green eyes find mine. Then his arms are around me and I find safety in the crook of his neck, enveloped in the pine scent of his hair, comforted in the strength of his hands.

The snow falls. The wind blows. This is Wonderland. It's perfect. It's love. It's *home*.

White rabbits all the way down.

ACKNOWLEDGMENTS

To Marcia Ruiz-Olguín thank you for being my fearless editor, my most trusted story advisor, the most stunning cover artist, and the greatest friend I've ever known.

To Katy Doyle thank you for tolerating my nonsensical use of semicolons and Taylor Swift references while proofreading my work. And thank you for being a constant support through the stress and madness my chaotic storytelling creates.

To Jay Gaunt thank you for always cheering on my writing, even back when I had no confidence in it myself—*especially* then. And thank you for lending your name to these pages, the world has Jay Dove because of your generosity.

To my hype team: Ali, Amanda Nikole, Fern, Mika, and Roslyn thank you for all the online support and positive energy, you make the creation process so much more invigorating.

To my mother thank you for your endless support and love.

And to Ashley and Eric thank you for being there during the darkest days, may we meet again someday on friendlier tides.

ABOUT THE AUTHOR

Molly Likovich is the #1 Amazon Bestselling Author of *Riding The Headless Horseman*. She holds a BA in Creative Writing from Salisbury University and her individual poems and short stories have appeared in numerous magazines and literary journals. She currently lives in the far off land of Maryland with her family and some friendly ghosts.

www.ingramcontent.com/pod-product-compliance
Lightning Source LLC
Chambersburg PA
CBHW060505300726
48975CB00008B/2661